My Joy
By
Christian Cashelle

My Joy
By Christian Cashelle
A Dynamic Image publication

Other titles by
Christian Cashelle:

Gino's Revenge

Ava's Story

When All Else Fails

Revisions of Life

Birds in the Rain: A poetry collection

Erika, our struggles will liberate others. You just have to believe in the talent God has given you. Thank you for helping me with this project.

5th Avenue Dreams

A familiar tune crept through the air waves as the sun beamed through the blinds that were half way opened. It was God's way of waking nineteen-year-old Camryn Lacey up from the peaceful slumber that engulfed her ever maturing body. Her eyes opened, sleep still written over her face as the events of last night replayed in her mind. She grinned as she turned her head to see Gino, the potential love of her life lying on his stomach beside her still sleeping. Her soft index finger traced his nose and his chiseled facial features as his brows furrowed. His eyes slowly opened seeing Camryn's heart warming smile as the start of his day. Surprisingly, he smiled back.

"Wassup, momma?" He asked, with slumber in his voice. All she could do was giggle. The mood was still set from last night, a night to remember. Camryn inhaled the almost present memory as Gino slipped back into sleep with his arms wrapped around her. The night started off rather chaotic, with Gino coming in her home with an attitude that she could barely stand. It was something about his stolen profit, he was short a few hundred dollars and he was trying to figure out who robbed him.

The Previous Night

"Are you sure it's missing, Gino?" Camryn asked with her arms around him, trying to calm him down.

"Yeah, I'm sure. That's money that I'm not going to have and you know that I

don't play with my money." He reminded her with a devilish scowl painted on his face. It was nine o'clock at night when he came tearing up her steps seeking someone to vent to about his financial woes.

"I'm sure you can make it all back by tomorrow. Watch, you won't even miss it." Camryn assured as she placed herself on his lap. Gino rubbed his face down as he blinked hard with frustration. "Trust me. You'll make it all back tomorrow." She reassured, caressing his tattooed arms. Gino was still agitated by the mystery as his mind scattered to who could have robbed him. Everyone in his camp was trusted with confidential information. There was a shark hiding somewhere amongst them.

"Calm down, baby." Her sweet voice almost sang in his ear as their eyes met each others as she placed small pecks on his lips. He could feel the anger slipping from his nerves at her gentle touch. Rising off of his lap, she grabbed a hold of his hand as he stood up following her unspoken command with bedroom eyes full of sensual anticipation. All of a sudden, his missing money escaped his mind as his attention was diverted to Camryn's curvy frame switching in front of him.

Entering the bedroom, he swung her around, his lips clashing against hers with a sensational feeling sweeping their bodies. The desire to make love fell on them like a weight. The night was inevitable. Gino knew he wouldn't be returning to his girlfriend tonight, reluctantly leaving his clandestine lover behind once again to wallow in oblivion. French kissing, he guided her to fall softly on her back onto the bed as he began to plant kisses all over her, barely having the patience to give Camryn the perfect foreplay. Camryn reached up removing the black tee over his head, exposing a clean wife beater that was leaving his body at an alarming rate also. Their lips were still entangled with a loving grip to accomplice; wrapped up in pleasure as their bodies were soon free of clothes, exposed to one another.

Usually, their love making involved a large magnum to provide protection, but as the passion made them lose sense, that wasn't even an issue. Placing himself between her delectable thighs, Gino's love muscle entered Camryn making her back arch. The way it felt was delightful, everything she was craving for at the moment he obliged. Her decorative nails clung deeply in his dark hazelnut skin as he took her body into consideration; pleasuring the both of them. His face, which was previously snuggled into her neck, was now watching her face twist up with contentment, providing Gino the confidence that what he was doing was feeling good. Camryn started to lose herself in the moment winding her hips to the rhythm that Gino gave as intense pleasure filled their bodies. There was nothing like good love to rid you of the world's struggles.

They reached the remnants of the first climax with no forewarning that this one moment lost in passion would change their lives forever. This moment would be eternally embedded into her memory though she was far from sense at the moment. Reaching climax, the love was unleashed from Gino, juices swimming up to meet and greet the nation that would form from inside of her loins. They would lie and make love for the rest of the night, thus leading them to forget about others and their wandering minds.

Now Present

Gino still lie spread about in her covers sleeping away the morning as Camryn opened her Biology book to study more about the many functions of cells for an upcoming test. You could never go wrong with intense preparation. She would be attending the community college to stay here and tend to family needs.

Her senses heightened as she heard Gino come alive once again. Camryn turned around to greet him with her eyes. He was shirtless exposing his hard rigid body, showing the effects of heavy weight lifting. He looked up at the clock as it read ten o'clock. Gino hopped up as his phone lit up, silently. For the fifth time, it was Tameka. He had better gotten home before she blew a gasket. He tossed the Carolina Blue covers back wiping his face and grabbing his clothes, dressing at once.

"You're gone?" Camryn asked. All he did was nod as he buckled his jeans heading over to where she was. He fit his white tank top over his head, grabbing his tee shirt to throw over his shoulder. He bent down and kissed Camryn on the lips as she smiled, watching Gino head out of the door.

Gino arrived at his comfortable brick house as he could smell the embers of a black and mild cigar sashay up his nose letting him know that Tameka, his actual girlfriend, was wide awake. Gino opened the doors to the cozy place he called home seeing Tameka leaning on the bar in the kitchen staring intently at him with the cigar perched between her fingers.

"So why did you decide not to come home last night?" She asked, inhaling the toxic smoke to calm her nerves. She was clearly livid, standing there with her satin head wrap on. Her oriental shaped eyes were glossed over as Gino leaned against the door.

"You know why I didn't come home last night. I had money troubles and I had to get that straightened out. You call yourself questioning me?" he asked with a sneer.

"I have the right to question you. You could've called and said you'd be out all night, Gino." she informed, stepping out of the kitchen. "I'm your woman; the least I deserve is to know where you are and what the hell you're doing!" Her octaves raised a height that Gino didn't find presentable. This was his house and no one was going to tell him when to come and go.

"Let me ask you something, Tameka?" He said rubbing his hands together. "Who pays the rent here? Who gave you the luxury of not having to work? Who provides for you and gives you money to buy the clothes and hair that you want? It's me, correct?" He smiled sarcastically. "That means I own all of this, including you. You have no right to ask me about anything." He said as Tameka's face grew hot. He was right and there was no telling him otherwise.

Tameka stood still, her feelings severed as he basically told her that she was like his dog. Dogs didn't have to work and had not a care in the world except its own well being. Though Gino said he loved her sometimes, he treated her as if she was nothing but a product of him. Long ago she would talk back, but nowadays, Gino had worn her down so much that she saw no use in trying to be smart with him. Ever since Gino's street credibility had risen exponentially, he had been changing. He stayed out later, and would come home and not touch Tameka at times. That made her wonder, but who wouldn't wonder? Leaving the small argument in the wind, Tameka eagerly followed Gino to their room as she ignited her daily conversation. There was one desire that Gino didn't want to meet, but she was determined.

"You still haven't given me an answer on having a baby. I just think it's time we try." She smiled uneasily, hoping for a polite answer with the word 'yes' running around in it. Gino, slightly confused at the quick turn in her mood, looked her in the face and shook his head.

"No, Meka. I'm not about to knock you up right now. Everything is dangerous and I don't need anything to dent my bank account anymore than you already are. Like I said the last time, you and I both aren't ready for a kid. Babies are expensive." He said kicking his shoes off.

"But Gino, my maternal instinct has kicked in and I would love to have something to love and I want something that we can share. The child could be like a symbol of our love."

"Look, I'll buy you a little dog, okay. We've talked about this a million times. Tameka we're not having a baby right now." He said pressing the activation button on the television remote. "End of story, no babies."

Tameka sighed and shook her head, furious of her unsuccessful attempts to convince Gino to have a baby with her. He knew how badly she wanted a bundle of joy, but Gino detested each time she brought it up. In Tameka's eyes she was ready for a baby, but Gino wasn't. She didn't think he ever would be.

Camryn's door creaked open as she put her book down and she saw her best friend's huge smile was plastered across her face.

"Hey, Cam." Mia greeted in a jovial mood as she outstretched her hands for a hug. Camryn reached up with a laugh and greeted her best friend with a hug as she saw the right side of her bed in a wreck. She could smell the faint cologne and it smelled just like Gino.

"Oh, I see Gino was here," Mia said rolling her eyes and taking a seat on the edge of the bed.

"Come on, Mia don't start." Camryn shook her head at Mia's obvious hate for Gino.

"I don't understand. That dude is going nowhere in life. Camryn what are you going to do when you start growing and he just stays the same old drug dealing, mob boss wanna-be? Okay, you love him right now and you think he loves you, but do you really think he's going to stick around. You deserve much better." Mia wagged her finger in front of her face, rolling her neck full of attitude, pronouncing her words diligently. "Out of all the men running around here, you choose Gino? That baffles me, why would you choose, Gino?"

Camryn fiddled with her pencil as she shrugged her shoulders, beginning to feel guilty about her romantic choices. Gino was good to her, even showering her with little gifts. He even gave her the money for her books for the summer classes. Camryn saw a side of Gino that no one else saw. He wasn't the menacing drug lord controlling the streets while he lay beside her in the bed, or laid on her chest for comfort. He was completely different, but no matter how many times she attempted to explain that to Mia, she would never understand it.

"I really wish you were coming to college with me. It would be so much better, but your grandma needs you around. I'd do anything to get you away from here," she said looking outside the window seeing one of Gino's many employees already hard at work. "I mean, look at that. Who wants to be stuck in mediocrity like that, just being one of Gino's little men? These dudes have so much more potential and so do you. I wanna get out of here. I can hardly wait to leave for college." She aired for the ninety-fifth time that week.

Camryn was starting to get annoyed by her constant boasting, but she knew how hard Mia worked for her education. She had earned the bragging rights. "I'll see if I can find you another man." She shook her, half-joking.

"I'm getting an education too and soon enough I'll have my degree and I won't be in debt from owing too much money from college. I'll get mine, I just so happen to be staying here," Camryn explained, smiling at her friend who was pampering herself in the mirror.

It's funny how we have everything planned out, but we have no way of seeing the future at all. We go through our days, as early as our childhood, planning out our lives and if we knew better we would plan, but not forget that we only have a limited hand on our future. God ordains the rest. In the back of our heads we know it's true, but it's up to us to acknowledge it. Life would go so much smoother if we did.

Breeding a Destiny

Camryn's sleek arms clung to her sides as she walked down the dimly lit hallway. The smell of medicine and rubbing alcohol filled her nostrils as she quickly made her way towards room 2344. Passing several rooms with lone patients, she wondered why no one came to visit them. She envisioned the relatives of these sickened souls were wealthy and selfish snobs who thought nothing of the wise ones who came before them. She could never do her Nana like that.

As Camryn came upon her destination, she could hear the jovial, yet raspy voice that warmed her heart many of days. Once she heard a separate voice, which she recognized to belong to her Nana's favorite nurse, she stopped at the door not to disturb their current conversation.

"Now you make sure that old man next door does not disturb me. You know I have several admirers around here but I need my rest." Camryn smiled to herself knowing that statement was nothing unusual for her grandmother to say.

"I sure will, Miss Marie. You make sure you get some rest today," the nurse replied. Camryn took this as her opportunity for a mediocre entrance and slightly tapped on the wide open door. A round-faced, caramel colored woman with beautiful gray hair looked towards Camryn as did the small Caucasian nurse standing next to her grandmother's bed. Her granddaughter's presence instantly brought a smile.

"There's my baby doll," Miss Marie stated while the nurse greeted Camryn. She slid her chocolate brown coach bag onto the blue chair up against the wall before embracing her grandmother in a hug.

"How are you feeling today, Nana?" Camryn asked with a strong hint of concern lacing her voice. This had been her grandmother's second hospital visit in three months but she tried to be strong knowing that her Nana was. The nurse quietly made her way out of the large, cold room and closed the door to give the two some privacy.

"Child, will you stop worrying. I'll be fine," Nana replied. Camryn let out a deep sigh. The pounding headache that she had developed earlier that day in her English class was proving to be immune to the painkillers she had taken not even two hours ago. "Cam, what's on your heart?"

"I'm just stressing about classes, Nana I'm fine," Camryn lied straight through her teeth. Her glossy eyes looked down onto the hard mattress where the one person she had depended on all of her life laid. It pained her more and more every time she came to visit this God-awful place. How could a place that was suppose to be a haven for the sick, feel so deadly?

"Nana, when are they going to let you come home?" Camryn repeated the question she asked every time she stepped foot into the room. Nana slid her fragile hand over her granddaughter's face before a warm smile spread across hers, lighting up her dark hazel orbs.

Miss Marie sighed knowing that her condition would never go away; only less painful on certain days. The autoimmune disease she had developed merely five years ago known as Lupus had governed her free will ever since. Her frequent hospital trips were tiring, but she made sure to put on a brave face for her baby. Several different illnesses had made their way into Miss Marie's system, the focus of this particular visit happened to be a blood clot.

"I'm not sure baby doll, but stop working yourself up about it," Miss Marie said gently patting Camryn's hand. "Nana is fine."

Camryn gave her Nana a forced smile knowing that would only half satisfy her. She knew that Nana was more worried about Camryn's mental health than her own physical. The complete truth was that Camryn felt physically sick from worrying about her grandmother. This had been her longest hospital visit in the last year or so. Every time she was admitted, Camryn feared she wouldn't come home. The thought alone brought her to tears because Nana was all Camryn had in the world, besides Mia and Gino, of course.

"So, how are your summer classes going?" Miss Marie inquired trying to lighten up Camryn's mood.

"They're good, only a few more weeks and I'll be done with this session." Camryn beamed. She was proud of herself for getting things done. During her freshman year, she had decided to take summer courses so that she would get her Associate's degree quicker. That was around the same time that Mia had announced that she was transferring to a university two and a half hours from home. Gino had protested against her taking summer courses. Camryn knew he was worried that she wouldn't have much time for him.

"Is Mia gone?" Nana asked and Camryn slightly shook her head no.

"She leaves in a few days. I'm actually going to help her pack after I leave here," Camryn responded. Miss Marie stared inquisitively at her only grandchild and wondered why Camryn couldn't realize that she knew that she was hurting. Camryn masked her pain to others well but never was Nana ignorant to Camryn's agony. She knew every scar, every bruise, every bump, and every heartache that Camryn had in her nineteen years of living. Miss Marie's intuition told her that Camryn was feeling down about Mia leaving. Selfish thoughts of telling her to stay were running through Camryn's head but she knew that she couldn't defer Mia's dream. That wouldn't make her much of a best friend.

"Um, I just know you better have my house spotless when I get home," Miss Marie warned while also trying to lift the deadly silence that had fallen upon the two. Camryn smirked before a small giggle escaped her lips. If it was one thing that she knew for sure, her Nana would always be… Nana.

"Yes ma'am," Camryn replied before standing upright and grabbing her purse. "Do you want anything on my way back?" Camryn asked letting her know that she would be back that afternoon.

"No child, I'm fine," Miss Marie replied as Camryn proceeded to place a tender kiss onto her smooth, yet cold forehead. The temperature of her skin caused a frown to play across Camryn's face.

"You need to get under this cover, Nana," Camryn demanded while raising the thick wool blanket up to her grandmother's neck. Miss Marie slightly rolled her eyes but obeyed Camryn's wishes and held onto the scratchy material with both hands. "See you when I get back. I love you."

"And I love you."

Mia slid her hand through her rough ponytail as she flopped down on her bed, pushing a few small cardboard boxes out of her way. Although she was excited about her move to an actual university, packing up her belongings had to be the only regret she had. Mia hadn't realized all of the clothes and shoes she owned. She knew she couldn't possibly take everything, so she had divided her room into three sections. One section was what she was taking with her, one was staying there and the other would be given to Cam.

Mia was excited, nervous, and upset all at the same time. She knew there wasn't much in this town for her, so her excitement lay in the fact that she was trying new things and leaving a dead end place. She was nervous because although she felt she was bigger than this town, the fear of failure lingered along side of her ambitions. She wanted so badly to make her mother and father proud of her that she often lost sight of her own dreams. Her being upset all tied into her relationship with her best and maybe even only friend Camryn. Mia and Camryn had been tight since their last year of junior high and what brought them so close was their identical dream of getting out. They were always together up until the time they turned 17 at the beginning of their senior year in high school. That was when Gino, a well known dealer, took an interest in Camryn. Mia would never abandon her, but she knew that their relationship had suffered at the large hands of Gino.

Just as Mia was securing one of the many boxes with a large strip of gray masking tape, a slight tap on her door filled her ears.

"Mia, its Cam," the familiar voice called from the opposite side. Without approval, Mia's wooden door slowly swung open to reveal her best friend. A smile was given by both parties, which was a common non-verbal welcome between the two.

"Looks like a tornado ran through here, boo," Camryn joked slightly moving a filled open box out of her path with the toe of one of her black low-top forces. Mia smirked at the comment before moving the box in front of her over to the stack of completely full boxes that were up against her closet door. Taking another glance at Camryn, Mia realized that the light denim skirt she was wearing belonged to her. Camryn followed her eyes and smirked.

"What, you want it back right now?" Camryn half heartedly asked. Mia laughed.

"You can have that short thing, along with everything in that box," Mia replied, pointing to a box on her almond dresser that she had set aside for the things she was giving to Camryn. A squeal of excitement escaped Camryn's lips as she moved over to the box and rummaged through it. Camryn had always admired Mia's fashion sense and the fact that she had the means to satisfy her addiction. Most of Camryn's money had gone to paying Miss Marie's hospital bills and pharmacy subscriptions. When Gino gave her pocket change, as he called it, she usually ended up spending it on school supplies, things for the house, or groceries.

"You sure you want me to have all of these things?" Camryn asked.

"Cam, please don't start," Mia warned as Camryn threw both of her small arms up in a mock surrender.

"Okay, okay."

For the next hour or so, Camryn assisted Mia in the mission of getting her things ready for the next chapter of her life. All the while, Camryn wondered when her current chapter would end and would she face new endeavors.

"I've been thinking, after I get my associate's, I might come up there with you," Camryn commented in a nonchalant way. An airy gasp escaped Mia's mouth as Camryn playfully rolled her eyes.

"Are you serious?" Mia asked more excited than she should be.

"It was just a thought Mia, don't get carried away." Camryn warned her.

"I'll accept that for now."

"Even though I'm not ya man, ya not my girl. I'ma call you my, shawty."

Just as Mia's hopes were raised, the ring tone that sounded from Camryn's Samsung M300 crushed them. She knew not to say anything about Camryn and Gino's so-called relationship unless she wanted another argument.

Giddy about her incoming call and oblivious to her best friend's distress, Camryn quickly pressed talk on her phone with a huge smile on her face.

"Hey," She answered in a seductive voice as Mia began to tune her out. She felt it would be best if she didn't hear the content of the conversation because it would only upset her more. Most of her things were packed, all except what she would be using for the next few days, so she began to move the boxes closer to the wall and out of the way.

About five minutes later, Mia heard Camryn flip her phone shut.

"Let me guess, you're leaving?" Mia said with little emotion. Camryn frowned as she wondered why Mia always did this. Why couldn't she see that Gino was making her happy? "You know that he's still messing with Tameka."

Her statement had immediately caused anger to rise in Camryn's eyes.

"That's not true. She's still after him and he's told her that he wants nothing else to do with her so you're tripping," Camryn replied quickly causing Mia to stand up straight and look her dead in her eyes.

"Are you serious, Camryn Charmaine? Do you really think that's the truth?" Mia asked, raising her voice an octave higher than it was.

"Yes, I do."

"Why? Because Gino said so? You are so naïve," Mia said shaking her head realizing that hope was slowly diminishing for getting Camryn to see the truth. Camryn, obviously hurt by her best friend's insult, sucked her teeth.

"You know what, Mia? I would really appreciate it if you tried to act happy for me. I didn't say anything about you up and leaving me now did I? No, I didn't. So act like you understand just a little about your best friend and try to act like you care." Camryn's scratchy voice came through causing Mia's eyes to soften.

"Okay, Camryn." Mia spoke softly.

"Do you have things you need to do?" She asked and Mia nodded. "Well, come drop me off at the hospital and you can have the car," Camryn said picking up her purse and sliding her sock clad feet back into her forces.

"How are you going to get…nevermind," Mia said waving off her own question and following her best friend out of the room. Mia shook her head as she realized all the growing up they had left to do. Although she didn't agree with Camryn about the dysfunctional relationship between her and Gino, she knew that she could no longer intervene. Camryn would have to learn on her own.

Gino slid the tightly re-rolled Black and Mild from his lips as his black 2006 Cadillac CTS pulled up in front of the emergency entrance to Mercy Hospital. Expecting

Camryn to be outside, he lifted his black Sync from its holding place and dialed the unsaved number. Fortunately, before he pushed the talk button to initiate the call, Camryn came hastily out of the automatic sliding doors and through his passenger door. She placed her small hand over her chest as she tried to catch her breath. Gino's nose flared a little before he quickly pulled off, causing Camryn to reach for the seat belt.

"Are you okay?" Camryn quizzed as she noticed his dark demeanor.

"What took you so long?" He asked, completely ignoring her question. Camryn bit her lip almost forgetting how impatient Gino could be.

"Nana's doctor wanted to talk to me about when she could come home," Camryn said. Although for that quick moment he sympathized with Camryn, his mind quickly switched back to his current dilemma at hand. "Baby, what's the matter?" Camryn asked one again while slowly running the manicured nail on her left index finger over the edge of Gino's ear. His phone ringing interrupted them before he could vent his current frustration to Camryn.

"What up?" He answered.

"The boy isn't back yet," the caller explained causing the thick vein in Gino's neck to pop out even further.

"How long has it been?" Gino asked. The caller explained that the delivery boy had departed around noon. Gino gently shook his head as he glanced at his yellow gold, diamond-faced Bulova watch which read 3:15.

"He should have been back before one."

"Find him," Gino commanded before hanging up. He then made a sharp turn onto Camryn's street.

"What happened?" Camryn asked cautiously. Gino licked his full bottom lip as he turned the key in the ignition and the engine died down.

"People are trying to get killed."

Camryn took pride in the fact that she knew just how to tame Gino's anger. She knew exactly what to do and was sure that no one else could do it better. Camryn smirked as she thought about Gino's ex, Tameka.

Before Gino ended it with her, Camryn had spent many nights un-doing the damage Tameka had done on that particular day. He even joked about Camryn being his personal stress reliever. Now that Tameka was out of the picture, Camryn knew that it was just a matter of time before she could have Gino exclusively. Thoughts of being known around town as his girl filled her head and caused her to smile.

As Gino vented about the disorganization and lack of loyalty in his camp, Camryn took it upon herself to warm up the lasagna she had made the night before. Loading his plate with the delicious pasta and two slices of Texas Toast, Camryn strutted into her cozy living room and set the plate down in front of him. She then retreated back into the kitchen, poured him a tall glass of soda and went back into the living room.

"You're not eating?" Gino asked as he noticed Camryn watching him while he ate. She gently shook her head no before making herself comfortable against the arm of leather couch.

"I don't have much of an appetite," she explained before receiving a head nod.

As she waited for Gino to finish his meal, Camryn closed her eyes as she began to feel a slight headache forming on the left side of her head. She assumed that it was a direct result of all the studying she had been doing lately. Her classes were beginning to get a little difficult but she knew she couldn't over do it. The air circulating through the room began to lull Camryn to sleep as she grabbed a small red blanket and covered up with it. Almost into a deep slumber, Camryn was stirred by Gino's smooth hand caressing her exposed thigh. She smirked as her senses began to intensify as he placed his knee on the couch and hovered over her.

"Aren't you supposed to be cheering me up?" he asked before Camryn took her small hands and slid the black sun glasses off of Gino's smooth face and placed them onto her maplewood coffee table.

"I got this," Camryn said repositioning herself so that she was now in the dominant position, straddling Gino's lap.

After every article of clothing was removed, a light curse arose from Gino's lips as Camryn bit her own while slowly rocking her hips in a teasing manner. Gino knew that his anger wouldn't allow him to take it slow, so he firmly gripped Camryn's full hips and began to accelerate his rhythm. Camryn threw her head back in an attempt to suppress the pleasure, but was met with unfamiliar knotted feeling in her abdomen.

"G," she spoke softly but the distant look in his eyes told Camryn that he didn't hear her at all. She swallowed some saliva trying to fight the urge to vomit. Gino slammed into her and Camryn felt as if he had pushed it up from her stomach and out of her mouth. She quickly jumped off of Gino, running towards her bathroom while chunks of things she had consumed at an earlier date spewed through the small space between her fingers while her hand held most of it in. She could hear Gino cursing as she finally made it to the toilet.

"What the hell is wrong with you?" A naked Gino yelled disregarding the fact that she was slumped over the toilet. He violently grabbed the closest towel and began to scrub at his arm where a small measure of vomit lay. Before Camryn could respond, Gino had her on her feet and pinned to the wall by her neck. An expression of shock and fear graced Camryn's face as Gino repeated his question.

"I'm sorry," Camryn cried out as Gino's face softened and he let her go. He then commanded her to sit down as he ran some hot water over the golden-colored, cotton face towel that sat next to the sink. Camryn sighed as he handed it to her.

"Wipe your face off." He spoke with no emotion as Camryn glanced up at him then back down at her feet in embarrassment.

Camryn sighed in aggravation as she waited for her name to be called. After what she did last night, Gino insisted that she go to the doctor. She knew nothing was wrong with her but she went anyway.

Her frustration also stemmed from Mia leaving a few hours ago. They had laughed, cried and said their goodbyes after Mia made Camryn promise to visit soon. It hadn't really hit her that her best friend was leaving until she saw her drive off. Camryn was very proud of Mia, all things considered. She knew this small town was full of dead end dreams and she was happy that Mia had found her way out. Not everyone's path was the same though.

"Camryn Lacey?" A nurse asked looking around the small waiting room after sticking half of her body out of the white door. Camryn grabbed her purse and walked over to the nurse and smiled at her. "How are you today, Camryn?"

"I'll be fine as soon as I leave here," She responded honestly, causing the nurse to let out a little laugh. Camryn followed the short nurse down a hallway that held several closed doors.

"You'll be in room 3," the nurse explained as she stopped in front of the corresponding door. "We'll need you to disrobe and put this on and the doctor should be in shortly." The nurse handed Camryn the paper thin dress with the back exposed and opened the door for her.

Camryn sighed as she waited for the nurse to close the door. She hated taking off her clothes for these check-ups. She quickly undressed herself and put on the proper attire. Standing on her toes, she gripped the edges of the examination table and pulled herself onto it in a sitting position. After a few minutes, a slight tap on the door was followed by Dr. Adams coming in with a smile on her face.

"How are we today, Miss Lacey?" Dr. Adams asked while glancing at Camryn's file. Camryn gave her a simple answer before being instructed to place both feet into the holders and lean back. "You know how this goes so try to remain relaxed and I'll get this done as quickly as possible." Camryn nodded as she released a deep breath and tried not to think about the woman who was inserting a metal opener into her at the moment. What seemed like minutes later, Dr. Adams announced that she was all done.

"Is that all you need?" Camryn asked ready to leave as soon as possible.

"Yes, although the initial general results usually take about fifteen minutes to develop. If you would like to wait in here for the results, that will be fine." The doctor announced.

"General results?" Camryn asked.

"General results are sexually transmitted infections, pregnancy, that sort of thing. That was what the blood and urine sample was for earlier."

"Okay, that's fine," Camryn said waving it off. The doctor exited the room, giving Camryn privacy to get dressed and discard her examination gown. Exhausted from the events of the past few days, Camryn lay back on the table and closed her eyes while she waited for the doctor's return.

"Miss Lacey?"

Camryn's eyes fluttered before she quickly sat up realizing she had dozed off.

"I'm sorry I'm a little tired," Camryn explained but the doctor waved her off with a smile. Camryn began to slide her shoes back on as she prepared to leave.

"It's fine, perfectly normal considering your condition."

"Considering my condition?" Camryn asked wondering what was wrong with her.

"The general results showed that you are about seven weeks pregnant."

Camryn froze after the word pregnant was received by her brain. Words weren't formed and all movement was lost causing a frown to lie on Dr. Adam's lips.

"Miss Lacey, are you okay?" She asked slowly waving her hand in front of Camryn's dazed face.

"Um, are you sure?" Camryn asked not believing what she had just heard. Dr. Adams' face turned into one filled with empathy as she handed Camryn the results. Camryn's mouth dropped as she read over it, putting the simple words together that resulted in something so complex.

Just when you assume that you have everything in your life under control, God gives you something to think about. Something happens that has to break you down so that He can build you back up in His image, how He wants you to be. Not everything is going to go your way.

Camryn lay stiff on her queen sized bed with her knees bent causing her legs to slightly twist underneath her. Her small hands were tightly entangled into her hair. The thought of breathing came difficult to her as she lay with her eyes wide open looking at the textured off-white ceiling.

The ceiling fan whirled as she finally closed her eyes slowly to try and ease the pain of the migraine she got once she left the doctor's office. On the right of her lay a small business card with a date within the next week to rid her of this current tragedy. Camryn couldn't be a mother. She could barely take care of herself.

With a solution in play, Camryn now set her worries on making sure that Gino did not find out. She recalled several of his frustrations with Tameka were stemmed from her wanting to have a baby. Camryn did not want to create problems between her and her lover, especially not within her quest to become his woman.

Minutes turned into hours as Camryn drifted off to sleep as a melodic tone filled her ears while drowning out the hum of the ceiling fan. Camryn's right hand unconsciously slid across her stomach as visions of a mother and her son flashed through her mind and before her eyes.

The painful joy of giving birth, the excitement of first steps and first words flew by as well. Scenes flashed of graduations, birthdays, and just warm, unforgettable moments between a boy and his mother. They slowly disappeared, dissolving into space, as an angelic face very similar to Camryn's mother's appeared crying. Camryn tried to call out to her but no words were audible. Through her tears, the angel smiled before placing her hand on top of Camryn's, causing a unique sensation to overtake her body.

"This child will thrive off of the ultimate strength that God has placed within your temple. He will bring light and unconditional joy into your life and will be your sole reason of living. You have been chosen to bless the world with a beautiful gift from God. He will do great things whether only in a small neighborhood or a whole nation. He has been conceived with a purpose and no one can stop it. You must protect this child with your life, Camryn Charmaine Lacey. You must accept this responsibility and receive your blessing. You have been chosen to perform a great task. Though it will take much patience, strength, and sacrifice you will be blessed with these qualities and more. Stay in prayer, love what you will become. His life deserves a chance."

Snapping out of her dream as well as her slumber, Camryn quickly sat up, placing her other hand over the one that lay protectively over her stomach. Salty tears streamed down her face as she looked around realizing what had just happened.

Point of No Return

Last night she got not an ounce of sleep, rocking herself like she was a newborn baby. It was as if the lightly colored walls were closing in on her all at once. The thoughts of her baby ran through Camryn's mind in blotches of movie clips every time she blinked or tried to drift off into slumber.

Camryn grabbed the neatly printed card that held the doctor's name on it and read the address for the fifth time contemplating if she would really go in the morning despite the frighteningly prophetic dream that she had. Was it real? Was it her conscious trying to speak to her? She knew Gino expressed his desire to remain childless and she'd do anything, even if it was underhanded and sneaky, to stay in his good graces.

For the first time, Camryn rolled her eyes at the break of dawn as the sun woke up the beings that inhabited the earth. It was time for a new day, and on this new day she was about to destroy a new life in just a few hours. The hours of early dawn crept by with gore underlying in its mood. Even though the sun shined, nothing was bright about this day.

She set her foot onto the concrete on Ebert Drive. Her appearance was still giving off the impression that everything in her life was a dream. She wore her favorite outfit, trying to hide the fear and uncertainty of this whole catastrophe. Walking into the chilly clinical office she took a look around at the people there. Some were sitting down with their hands in a praying position. Some had their eyes closed. This was the clinic, everyone that was here was convinced that something was abnormally wrong in their body, but was *this* baby wrong?

"Ms?" The clerk asked with the colorful scrubs on. Camryn looked her way and smiled, apologizing for her not paying attention. "Your name?"

"Lacey, Camryn Lacey."

"Insurance," she said in a polite tone. She handed her the Blue Cross Blue Shield health insurance card as she nervously tapped her feet, studded out in baby doll shoes, as she saw a girl walk out of the doors with tears staining her face. A guy walked up to her and threw his arms around her.

"You did what you had to, what were we going to do with a baby?" He asked, with a smile.

Camryn's heart twisted. It was obvious that the girl was broken up inside about killing her unborn child. Who was there convincing her that she didn't need the baby? Her boyfriend? Camryn turned her head from the sorrowful scene displayed as the nurse behind the desk gave her the card back.

"Someone will be with you shortly."

Camryn smiled politely and sat in the lobby beside a girl that looked like she was just hours away from death with shabby clothes and hair that hadn't been groomed that day. Her brown eyes were dim and morbid. Camryn wanted to reach out and touch her, but thought against it. She decided to mind her business, but as she closed her eyes and shook her head the young girl began to speak, it was sign number two.

"You know you're not supposed to be here." She smiled a smile that did not reach her eyes.

"Excuse me?" Camryn asked as she turned to her, clenching onto her purse.

"You're really going to let a man determine if a child that lives inside of you lives or dies?" Finally she looked at Camryn who was full of emotion.

"You don't even know me," she spoke, her lips quivering as hot tears made themselves more than visible.

"I don't have to know you. If you kill this baby, it's like killing yourself and you'll never be able to live with it." Camryn opened her mouth to plead her case as her name was called. She slowly rose from her chair as the girl's dark eyes followed Camryn over to the door that lead into what was about to take place.

"Okay, if you just disrobe and put this on, we can begin the procedure," she smiled heading out of the door.

Camryn sighed and began to remove her apparel as a baby's face flashed through her head smiling and laughing. An abortion felt like murder. The baby was innocent but she couldn't risk bringing a baby into the wrong time and the wrong place. Camryn planned to be married and have her degree when she had a child so the baby would be well taken care of. This baby would come when she had nothing together for herself. A mediocre job and only her second semester of college were the only things on her record.

Guilt plagued her bones, making her movements slow and rigid as the weird girl's words kept replaying like a scratched CD with the stop button disabled. She couldn't ignore it; it was loud like a siren. The doctor came in with a hopeful smile like they weren't ending a life. Camryn propped herself on top of the table as the doctor instructed her to put her feet up on the petals, instructing her on the process of the exam before the actual procedure. She thought about the fact she was in that very same position when she was given the news of her pregnancy not even a week ago and she closed her eyes.

"*He has been conceived with a purpose and no one can stop it*." She opened her eyes and looked down to the doctor as she washed her hands. Apparently, she hadn't said anything, but Camryn could hear the voice loud and clear. It was the same words that she heard in her dream. With her heart ferociously pounding in her chest, Camryn removed her propped up feet as she took long hard breaths.

"Ms. Lacey," the doctor rushed to her as she got up shaking her head.

"I'm sorry, I can't do it." She grieved as tears filled her eyes. "I can't kill this baby," she said. Camryn picked up her clothes, slipping her dainty feet back into her shoes. The doctor was left speechless as she hurried out of the door in a blur of a person, bolting through the doors.

Startled from the suddenness of the clinic's doors opening roughly, the nurse behind the desk jumped up as she reached for the phone.

"No, let her go." The doctor rushed out, signaling that it was fine. As
Camryn bolted out of the exit doors. The sunlight felt like freedom and the sun seemingly shined much brighter. It sent warmth and comfort to her skin as she sighed in relief. She inhaled the fresh air before looking for her car.

She cried from the mix of emotions as she hurried inside her car. Throwing her things in the passenger seat, Camryn gripped her steering wheel with both hands and cried.

Everything was seemingly well in Tameka's world as her slightly slanted, dark eyes traveled over the ruggedly handsome image of her man, who she based her life on. She moved the dyed strands of red tinted hair from her forehead as he carried her bags full of clothes in his strong arms. Gino's voice was quiet and calm as he held his phone up to his ear, briefly conversing with Twan, his business partner and best friend, who was handling some other business across town. After closing the phone shut, he looked over at Tameka's bedazzling eyes and smiled.

"What else does my baby want?" He asked, moving the bags to one hand and using the other to caress the small of her back. All she could do was grin from shining earring to earring as she giggled attractively. After all of this time, Gino still caused butterflies to erupt in her tummy.

"I got everything I want," she answered, the tip of her index finger grazing his hairless chin. Gino's eyes were fixated on another thing as Tameka looked in the direction and back at him to see him almost giggling like a child, his perfect healthy teeth were on showcase for every onlooker to see. Tameka's mouth fell open. Was he going to buy her what she would never in her life ask for?

They headed over to the man dressed immaculately in a shirt and tie with an overdone smile on his face. Tameka traced the clear glass in search of her newest prized possession as her orbs caught sight of a beautiful ring, its outer shell was all diamonds and underneath it was shimmering gold. Tameka's face rejoiced as she pointed to the ring.

"That one please." She smiled at the middle aged man as he unlocked the case letting her take a better look. Tameka glanced over at Gino, his eyes was scaling over the pricey ring itself.

"I like that, too. How much is it?" Gino wondered aloud.

"Um, it's about eleven hundred on sale." The man chimed in as if they couldn't afford such a rock. Gino dug into his deep denim pants pulling out a large stack of money and nearly tossing it across the counter. The salesman looked at the large stack amazed as he released its contents from the thick rubber band. Tameka pranced in joy as Gino retrieved the ring from the salesman after it was purchased and cleaned and slid it up on Tameka's finger. Her mouth, agape from the astonishing beauty before her eyes was priceless to Gino. Since he didn't want any kids at the moment, the least he could do to keep her mouth shut was to ice her up. Gino lifted her adorned face to match his level as he softly kissed her lips.

"I love you. Don't ever forget that shit," he advised with caution. Tameka nodded her head eagerly and smiled, throwing her arms around Gino, the one she hoped would be with her forever. Everything was all good, right? Walking out of the mall, Tameka held her hand in front of her, marveling the perfection of the diamond ring.

"Gino, this is so fly."

He said nothing as he opened the door for his lady. She smirked and bit her lip at Gino's courteous compliment. Slipping into the car, he flashed a toothy smile over to Tameka, seemingly happy. It's a little strange at how much people change their personalities and it made the people seem so counterfeit. Sure, she loved Gino, but which side?

Arriving back home to the comfortable brick house, Gino grabbed her bags of clothes, shoes, and other accessories and lugged them into the house while Tameka basked in the feeling of being pampered like a queen and having Gino worship her. It was only a small fantasy of hers knowing that this whole neighborhood worshipped

him and saw her as just Tameka, Gino's girl. The bags
made it to the bedroom as Tameka carelessly opened the
shoe boxes exposing her Nine West Pumps as she slipped
them on to her dainty feet admiring them. Besides Gino,
nothing else in the world mattered more to her than looking
and feeling prosperous, no credit given to her. The fine
tuning in her ear heard the water crashing against the tub,
not seeing the anticipating grin painted on Gino's features.

Gino removed his chain, along with his crimson LRG
shirt, making his way toward the master bedroom. Gino's
body was designed by an elite craftsman; his bulging
forearms, his chest, and his chiseled abdominal muscles
were enough to make a woman forget her manners.
Tameka's fresh manicure traced over his decorated skin,
with scenes of ink telling stories and reliving memories of
fellow fallen soldiers. While Tameka was heavily fixated
on his physical attributes, his hands were occupied in
slipping the six inch heels from her feet and ultimately
undressing her. She threw her head back in laughter as his
index finger traced up her curvy leg, eventually tickling her
as her chocolate frame appeared naked to the senses. His
hands massaged themselves happily over her bounteous
breast, slightly maneuvering her nipple as her back arched
inward at his intoxicating touch.

"Come on baby, I've got your bubble bath ready."
Gino leaned upright as he stuck his hand out for her to
grasp on to as he led Tameka to their romantic destination.

Gino bit his bottom lip with his eyes focusing on her
exquisite shape as it became one with his hand, causing a

small giggle to erupt from her mouth. She stepped over into the tub of bubbles and sat down slowly as she let her hand slip from Gino's. Backing away with an alluring smile, he unhooked his belt buckle, thus forth undressing himself. The water gathered onto her skin gladly as her eyes fell upon his body like a parachute. Her hands gripped lovingly on her skin as the water washed over her. Gino stepped into the tub as they repositioned themselves. Tameka sat between his legs as she relaxed into his arms, her head resting against his shoulder. Gino's hand moved slowly over her as the suds clothed her nakedness and Gino's rounded lips kissed upon her neck, trailing his fingers gently against her skin.

"Gino, I love you," her voice crooned sweetly in his ear as he looked her deeply in her eyes.

"I love you too, babe," He said, unattached from emotionalism. Tameka disregarded his voice, knowing that the talk of love troubled him for some reason. If she could, she would stay here for all of eternity with Gino, but she knew that the outside world would always beckon for them, especially him. Gino continued his conquest on her skin as he cupped the fresh water into his hands rubbing it upon her shoulders followed by kisses. If only, he would stay this genuine and this serene.

Nonetheless, the money spent treating Tameka was back into his pocket in half weeks time as he pushed end on his phone, disregarding making another phone call to someone who had not been returning the missed calls. He turned up his lip as he noted this among the many times that Camryn hadn't answered her phone. Was there somebody else better than Gino in her life?

The thoughts of her infidelity swarmed through his thought process in seconds as his anger rose in temperature. Pulling the clutch on his car, he headed down her street knowing that she couldn't ditch his presence like she did his calls. Slowly climbing out of the car, he made his way up the brick steps, opening the screen door upon ringing the bell.

"I'm coming," Camryn chimed heavenly from inside. Gino now knew that she was indeed home and became even more furious as his speculation was true, she had been avoiding him. Camryn opened the door, oblivious to who it was standing on the opposite side of the door.

"You've been dodging my phone calls." Gino stood at the threshold of her steps blocking her entrance.

"I'm sorry Gino. I just had to take some time." She lied still standing a few feet away from her lover.

"Time?" he questioned as he came down off of the steps. Gino walked around his young lover with a quizzical stare looking and searching for anything suspicious. "Do you have something you need to tell me?"

She wasn't going to tell Gino about the baby until later, but now must have been the right time because there was nothing she could do about what was coming.

"Gino, I think you should come inside for this." Camryn moved a stray hair from her face as Gino's

eyebrows rose at the stench of suspicion as his black
Timberland clad feet paced slowly up the steps as Camryn
made rigid walks. Her legs felt like ice at the anxiousness
of the conversation. The screen door creaked open as the
both of them stepped into Camryn's home as Gino made
himself as comfortable as he could get while Camryn paced
in front of him.

"Camryn, why the hell are you pacing?" He asked
with his brows furrowed as he sat up, resting his forearm on
his knee. Camryn halted her pacing and sat down in the
lazy boy across from Gino as she took a long sigh.

"Gino, do you remember when I threw up that one
night?" She asked twisting her fingers.

"Yeah I do, and why?"

"Well I was…I'm pregnant." Camryn put her head
down mentally in touch with Gino's emotions as rage and
shock enabled his body as he stood up. Camryn kept her
focus on the carpet.

"You're what?" He asked, his feet moving closer to
her. Gino's movements became swift and articulate with his
hands grasping her wrists as she winced in pain.

"Gino," she called out to him as if he were able to
give mercy. She began to squirm as her frightened eyes
were caught by his. The grimace he held on his face was
enough to murder as Gino tossed her to the couch and
charged over to where her shaken frame was located, her
hair slightly disheveled. "Gino," She called out to him
again. He was never known, to Camryn, to even react to
situations this way. She found her face, wet to her

fingertips, tears blemishing her face. In a blink of an eye, Gino, or what seemed to be him was kneeling in her face as if he were searching for a light.

"What you mean?" He whispered in a sinister voice with a snarl on his facial features. Fear had stricken a hard chord within her membrane as her arms wrapped around herself as protection. She found it hard to repeat the news once again. He closed his eyes briefly waiting for her answer, when silence overstayed its welcome, he stood up, the palm of his hand clashing with the thick strands that made up her hair, sending her back into the sofa, forcefully. "Answer my question!" His voice was thunderous, making a peaceful setting turn chaotic.

"I'm pregnant." Her head hung as low as the willow tree branches that hung out front as cold tears fell from her round eyes. Gino's hands gripped Camryn's shoulder as he yanked her to her feet, just millimeters from her face.

"You're getting an abortion."

The word abortion echoed through her mind as she remembered herself running out of the clinic in a shambles of tears. Though she was frightened of Gino, nothing could cause her to kill this child.

"No." Her feet planted stiffly on the ground, protesting against Gino's will as he turned his face back to her. His face was stuck in a questioning stare. He yanked once more as her knees bent in disobedience, digging her toes into the carpet to add traction causing it to be difficult to get from the house and to his car. Finally, his grasp was broken as she fell back onto the carpet, scrambling to her feet.

"I'm not going to a clinic. I'm keeping this baby." Strength that she knew not of arose from the pit of her consumed belly as her chin was upraised, showing that she was steadfast and unmovable. "This baby has a destiny and I'll be damned if I let anybody take it." Though tears fell down her rosy cheeks, they didn't compromise her strength not even a bit as her fist clenched into a ball. All Gino could do was stand there and look her deep into the brown eyes he once used to lust over daily. Now he sat and despised the day his penis ever felt the warmth of her accomplice.

"Destiny, Camryn? How does something that can't even see right now have a destiny?" Camryn's tender voice had gone mute, not seeing the reason for explaining it to him profitable. Carnal minds could never possess the knowledge that the spiritual mine possessed, so trying to open his mind would be like feeding a toothless baby meat.

"Gino, you would never understand, I don't expect you to, but there's no way in hell that I'm killing this baby." Her hand rested trustfully on her womb, even though it seemed as if nothing was there. Gino licked his lips, bedraggled by the herb that he smoked almost daily. He was confident in his evil deeds.

"You'll regret ever making that decision. As far as I know, that is not my child." Gino's voice differed from what he was feeling inside as anger boiled deeply. His voice was calm and promising as he turned on his heel, opening and slamming the door upon his exit. Camryn sat down and cradled her stomach for comfort, reminding herself that she was doing this for her baby. The way Gino had acted pained her in so many ways that even her emotions were speechless. She was alone. Mia was at college, Nana was sick, and now Gino had disowned her and her child. What now?

Twan set the half rolled cigar on the glass coffee table as his dark eyes locked on Gino who hadn't even lit his blunt yet. He sat close in proximity, but far away mentally as he stared into the atmosphere of Twan's quiet house.

"G?" He asked mild mannered as he put the lighter beside the stash of marijuana that looked similar to dead grass. Gino's eyes cut away from his own world as his face remained stoic.

"What?"

"You're too quiet. You're usually the one talking my head off while I smoke this weed. It ain't right if you ain't babbling." Twan chuckled, lightly scratching on his chin. Gino exhaled deeply and put his head back.

"I got some shit I need to tell you," Gino admitted, about to air the source of his current grievance.

"Well, damn. I'm listening."

"Tameka isn't my one and only."

"You ain't scared?" Twan said to himself. "I can change that."

Camryn smiled as she hopped out of her car to see the nurse rolling her grandmother out to the passenger seat. Seeing this day was more than a blessing to her. Nana climbed into the car with the help of Camryn and the nurse with a smile maintained beautifully on her features. Camryn jogged to the driver side, giddy and in a praiseworthy mood among seeing her Nana finally coming home. Everything that was spinning out of control seemed to stop momentarily. That meant the pregnancy, the argument with Gino, and whatever else was going to happen.

"How have you been doing, Camryn?" Nana asked, peering out at the sidewalks where people jogged, and some stood and talked.

"I-I've been fine." Camryn smiled uneasily, just grateful that her grandmother was here.

"Something is troubling you?" Nana turned to her granddaughter while Camryn kept her attention straight forward, knowing that if she locked eyes with her grandmother, she could figure it out. Camryn was already disappointed in herself, it would be worse if Nana would be disappointed. Camryn forced a smile as she glanced at her grandmother.

"I'll leave it alone for now," she said, turning her head back to the outside attractions. "But as soon as I think you're ready, you're going to tell me about, you hear?" She asked.

"Yes ma'am," Camryn retorted, her hands now trembling on the steering wheel.

When Camryn reached her destination with Nana in the passenger side, the air smelled of rain. The musty grey clouds loomed above their heads as Camryn stared at them. For some reason, thunderstorms always made her cringe and she had no real reason why. Camryn helped her grandmother to the house, opening the screen door before her.

"We're going to talk about this in the morning. It's so fresh on my spirit," she said, wrinkling up her eyes. The doctor said she'd be a little tired, so she was making her way to bed. Camryn set out to go and fetch the rest of her things.

Camryn noticed Twan's Cadillac parked out front. Her legs froze in their tracks as she searched around for the hefty nemesis. He was nowhere to be found so she went out to the car to grab the rest of Nana's belongings. As she opened the car door, she heard faint breaths behind her as a menacing snarl overtook Twan's face.

"Are you scared now?" He asked, not giving Camryn a chance to breathe a syllable. Yanking the thousands of strands of her hair into his fists, he brought her face to his, releasing thick saliva from his mouth. "This is what happens when you don't do what we say," he hissed, as he sent her tumbling into the side of her car. Her hands trembled as she wiped the spit from her face, daring to make an intrusive entrance inside of her mouth. She lifted her face coming to the eye of a fist, jabbing into her eye incessantly. Nonstop; he repeated this painful notion as she slid down to the eroding concrete, feeling the blood ooze from her left eye. Twan's heart rate began to escalate as he brought his Nike clad feet up, forcefully kicking her in her womb where an innocent little fetus had just gained life. There's no way with the kicking and the stomping into her womb that the little prince or princess could make it out alive.

Horrid cries fumbled out of her mouth, as she covered her stomach and curled up in a ball, taking violent head shots from Twan's shoe. All she wanted to do was take care of this child and protect it. Through all of the pain that she was enduring, all she could think about was her child. Never mind the blood seeping from her eye or her throbbing head and side, but she minded her womb. Her tiny form went limp as her tight grasp around her ankles went numb, her fingers releasing. She lay, slumped over near the middle of the street as Twan backed away, wiping the sweat from his brow, checking his surroundings and making a hasty escape from the crime scene. The work was done; he had the blood on his white tee to show for it. Did he feel anything? The answer was no. He would reply slyly: "It's just business."

12:08AM marks eight minutes past midnight as teenagers steal their parent's car hoping for a joy ride and the chance to fulfill sexual desires. Pulling out of the curb the oldest sister noticed a figure laid out in the street. Her heart races as she tastes the streets mild night air.

"Get back in the car," her sibling whispers, "Before Momma comes out here."

"No, there's somebody out there. She might be dead."

At the sound of the word dead, the opposing sibling makes a slow exit out of the car, as she turns the lights out. They make their way over to the faintly breathing body with bulging eyes, afraid of what they might see.

"Oh my God, it's Camryn! Go call 911!" The oldest said as the other girl frantically fumbled with her phone, her shaking hands dancing on the keypad.

"Is she dead?" She asked before the operator picked up.

"I don't know, but there's blood everywhere."

The concrete was stained with old crimson liquid. It had darkened, letting the girl know that she had been here for a while.

"Who would've done this to her?" She asked herself. Her eyes searched for answers as she looked back up to her sister, talking to the 911 dispatcher. She hung up the phone in relief, bending down to be beside Camryn who still wasn't showing any signs of consciousness.

"Is she going to be okay?"

"I hope." The young teen sighed.

Who knows, maybe Camryn's pain saved someone else's pain. For all we need, those two teenaged girls could've ended up experiencing something that they didn't need to experience; Camryn may have saved them.

The clock seemed to stand still. Everything crept by like molasses. Gino sat quietly studying the wall, awaiting Twan's arrival. The truth was he was nervous. The apartment was dimly lit as he sat trying to justify his reasons for threatening Camryn's life as well as the baby gaining life from her womb. Hours had passed as Gino stood up, pacing back and forth.

"That motherfucker said he'd be back." He said to himself through clenched teeth. The sound of the door opening made him turn and face his best friend. Nothing was said, the only thing read was body language. Gino noticed the blood on the tail end of Twan's shirt as Twan gave him a merciless grin.

"It's done," Twan said, removing the bloodied shirt from his body.

"Where is she?" Gino asked in an appeased tone.

"Laid out; a baby shouldn't give you any trouble, since there isn't one, I'm for sure," Twan said, reaching in the fridge for a Budweiser. It had taken a few seconds for Twan to recognize his friend's demeanor as Gino stood quietly, his hand resting above his chin, his back turned. It seems like Gino had finally caught a conscious.

"You weren't even sure if you wanted to do that, were you?" Twan asked, as Gino turned his face toward him.

"It had to be done," Gino snapped, as he let out a stressed sigh. Twan held his hands up in a surrendering stance as a smile decorated his face. "What if she's dead?" He asked seconds later, breaking the silence.

"She's not and why do you care? You're the one who wanted her out of your life anyhow. Are you having second thoughts, G'?" Twan asked, letting his words play torturous mind games. Twan knew that Gino hadn't thought this whole thing out, but it was mildly enjoyable to see Gino in discomfort. "Were you not sure?" He asked again.

"Fuck you!" Gino whipped around, catching wind of what Twan was doing to him. He pointed his finger in his face and slowly put it to his side as he closed his eyes. Twan had taken no offense to Gino's choice of words, all he did was snicker to himself.

"This should tell you, think before you do. You know that kid Camryn is innocent but you're not. You know that baby was innocent, but you're not. Camryn's guilty of what; loving you?" Twan said, as Gino's brows furrowed listening to the things that he had already told himself.

"Don't tell me what I already know. If she would've just gotten an abortion, none of this would have happened!" He yelled in distress.

"Yeah, but look what you got yourself into; a battered mistress and a dead baby."

"But you did it." Gino hissed back.

"But who had the motive? It's funny that you're playing the blame game now. You can't take it back. Unfortunately, you're not God." Twan spat. "Yeah, I did the dirt, but who created the dirt; you!" he said, his index finger indenting his choice. Gino's eyes grew solemn as he accepted the truth.

"It still had to be done." Gino reassured. "That's what happens when you don't listen."

This Can't Be Life

Tameka's dark pink tongue quickly slid across her white teeth as a smacking noise sounded from her lips. The loneliness from not seeing her man all day had finally gotten the best of her and within a matter of a half an hour, she was dressed in a simple black and red Lady Enyce warm up suit and some black and red Jordan's. Tameka tried calling Gino once more before her nostrils flared.

"I hate his ass," she uttered while violently grabbing her black Coach backpack purse and stomping all the way down their winding staircase and out of the kitchen door. Punching the code into Gino's black Lincoln, Tameka slid smoothly into the driver's seat before adjusting it. Making another call to a different number, Tameka smiled once someone picked up.

"Hello?" a squeaky voice answered.

"I hope you're at home because I'm around the block," Tameka spoke with an urgency to speak to another human being. Gino liked for her to stay in the house so Tameka rarely got to spend time with her friends.

"Um hum," the voice responded before hanging up. Thinking nothing of it, Tameka slid her white Sony Ericsson slider closed and pushed her foot farther onto the accelerator.

Less than ten minutes later, Tameka pulled up in front of a small house that appeared to be brick from the front but was siding everywhere else. There were two small kids playing in the front yard with a few destroyed toys. Tameka smirked as she punched in the alarm on the Lincoln before turning her small frame away from it. The young boy in the yard immediately stopped what he was doing and picked himself up off the ground. His short stumpy legs quickly carried him towards Tameka where his arms wrapped themselves around her right leg. A smile spread across Tameka's lips as she bent down to pick the boy up.

"How's my God son?" Tameka asked as the young boy's eyes sparkled at the sight of his loving Godmother.

"Meka, Jacob hit me!" The young girl exposed, causing Tameka to glare at the three-year-old in her arms. Jacob immediately became scared of Tameka's reaction and began to plead his case.

"Tia pushed me first, Meka!" He explained.

"You both know better." Meka warned before putting Jacob down and patting him on his butt. "Now, play nice before I make you both come in the house."

"Okay." The twins said in defeat as Tameka's confident stride carried her up the few concrete stairs and in front of the white door. Disregarding proper manners to knock, Tameka's small hand twisted the knob until it clicked before pushing her way into the house. A television personality filled Tameka's ears as he announced what the number five video of the day was. Her eyes fell to the high yellow female spread across the dark green couch. Her thick legs hung over the edge as she tapped her long gel nails on her thigh.

"What's up?" The woman greeted Tameka without looking away from the large television set. Tameka left the door cracked before taking a seat in the matching recliner diagonal from the couch. "Meka close the door, you are letting the air out."

"Lori, your kids are outside by themselves." Tameka frowned but her statement did not faze the woman opposite her.

"They are okay," she responded which caused Tameka to sigh. It wasn't as if Lori was a bad mother, she was just careless at times.

Although this was the case, Tameka wondered why God would bless someone like Lori with twins when she didn't even want kids in the first place. Tameka wanted a child so bad and it showed in her relationship with her best friend's twins. The twins adored Tameka and did whatever she told them to do. Everyone on the block often joked of them actually being Tameka's children instead of Lori's.

Lori was Tameka's best friend, you could say only friend. Growing up on the same block, Lori and Tameka did everything together from the time they met. Lori was a mix of black and white but only a few knew that. To everyone else she was just a regular red bone. Built up like a full blooded sister, Lori was shaped up like the girls on the videos, with an exception in the chest area. All the guys in their high school bragged that her ass made up for her short comings up top. Aside from their physical differences, Lori and Tameka were one in the same. Lori would claim to be smarter than Tameka in many ways but Tameka always thought she was naïve. Lori complained about Gino but her man was a drug dealer as well and on top of that, was locked up at the moment.

"Anyway, what are you doing on this side of town? You know your man doesn't like you over here," Lori joked with a seriousness that annoyed Tameka. Ever since high school Lori had gotten on Tameka's case about her dealings with Gino.

"I haven't even seen my man today," Tameka pouted, throwing her back into the recliner and sulking.

"Hell, go stand outside for ten minutes, he'll be through here." Lori laughed at her own joke. Tameka rolled her eyes in irritation causing Lori to give her an apologetic smile. "I'm sorry girl. I'm on one because Chase hasn't called me today," she explained and Tameka nodded in empathy, remembering the short time Gino had spent incarcerated a few years back.

"Isn't he getting paroled soon?" Tameka asked causing a smile to spread across Lori's dark pink lips.

"Girl yes, next month and can't wait!" Lori danced a little in her seat. "Plus, I'm tired of trying to explain to Jay and Tia where their daddy is."

As if hearing their names, the energetic twins ran through the screen door laughing as small angry voices came from the yard. Tia quickly closed the door as the two slid down it in a fit of giggles. Tameka gave Lori a puzzling look. Lori only shook her head.

"They are terrorizers, those kids next door be crying after they get through with them." She explained causing Tameka to quickly look at the two.

"What did you do?" Tameka asked in a stern voice that caused Jacob to look up at his older sister, by a few minutes.

"Nothing." Tia quickly covered as they took off towards the carpeted stairs. Lori laughed knowing that their attitudes and slyness came straight from her.

"It's not funny," Tameka said trying not to laugh as well.

"I'll stop laughing if you take them with you for the weekend," Lori said and Tameka nodded with quickness. Lori knew she really didn't even have to ask because Tameka came and got the twins often.

"Where is your hot ass going?" Tameka asked following after Lori to get the twins' things ready.

"Out," was Lori's reply which caused Tameka to smack her lips. "It's nothing Meka, stop tripping."

"Alright, Chase is going to flip when he hears about all the 'nothing' you've been doing." Tameka warned her best friend in concern.

"I am not worried about Chase."

Lori packed the twins what they would need and helped Tameka out to the car. Her breath got caught in her chest as she saw Gino's truck parked closely behind his Lincoln with him leaned against the trunk of it with Twan next to him. She unlocked the door with the remote attached to the keychain and Lori quickly walked her children to the back door. Tameka slowly made her way to Gino. He glanced at Twan and he walked around to the passenger side of the truck and got back in. Although she was upset with him, Tameka knew not to make a scene in public.

"What are you doing over here?" Gino asked as Tameka tried to see his eyes through his dark glasses.

"Baby, I got lonely so I came over to see what Lori was doing. Then Jay and Tia asked to spend the night," she explained herself as Gino sighed in irritation. He didn't have a problem with Jay and Tia spending the night but he knew Tameka would make every attempt to mention having a family of her own and he was not up for hearing that on this particular day. "Why haven't you checked on me today?" Tameka asked which caused Gino to quickly remove his glasses from his face as Tameka's lowered. Lori glared at the scene, seeing her best friend do a complete 180 for Gino almost made her sick.

"Call me when you want me to come get them," Lori said causing Tameka to look at her and nod. Lori looked Gino up and down in disgust before walking back into the house.

"I don't know why you insist on hanging with that hood rat."

"Gino," Tameka said letting him know this was a road far too much traveled. She had given up a lot of things for him, but Lori would not be one of them.

"Get to the house, Tameka. I'll be home in a couple." He said before making his way back to the driver's side of the truck, showing no affection to his woman whatsoever. Tameka sighed before getting in the Lincoln and turning around to face the twins.

"We buckled in?" She asked and they both nodded. "Alright."

How quickly we forget the things that seem to make us tick. Our heart beat falls when they aren't around yet we don't realize that every move we make has an effect on everyone around us. From children to significant others, we never realize that their preferences control us, in the most subtle way.

"Okay, what I would like you all to do for Wednesday is put a concrete topic for your next speech down on paper. Have your three main points as well and we'll work from there," Professor Matins spoke before dismissing her class. Mia frowned due to the excessive noise as rude kids put their things away early, causing intermission between her ears and the professor's words. She quickly grabbed her things and headed to her side.

"Excuse me, I couldn't hear what else you wanted us to have besides our topic," She asked looking down at the fresh piece of paper in her green notebook. The professor gave her a polite smile.

"You just need your three main points," she said. Mia nodded before jotting that information down in shorthand.

"Thanks," she said before making her exit from the large classroom. Brushing past a group of students, oblivious to the fact that they were blocking the entrance of the building, Mia made her way towards her car.

On her way to her off-campus apartment, Mia realized she was stressed. Not only did she miss home, the university experience was not what she pictured it would be. Although this was true, she decided to make the best of where she was. She also knew one of the reasons she was frustrated was because she had talked to Camryn all of three times since she had been gone. She hoped everything was well with her best friend. Mia wanted to be there for Camryn; in a way she could feel something wasn't right. She had her own issues at hand.

A smile spread across her face as she pulled up into her designated parking spot and saw her cousin, Jayson, making his way to his front door. Mia's aunt had gotten her this apartment because Jayson recommended it. Having a family member so close helped Mia get over her homesickness.

"Hey ugly!" Mia joked causing Jayson to turn around with a confused frown on his face. Upon seeing his younger cousin he rolled his eyes and turned back around to unlock his door.

"I don't see any mirrors out here, you better quit talking to yourself," he stated causing Mia to laugh as she followed him into his apartment. Jayson didn't react to

Mia's actions, as she always was at his place. He didn't mind unless he had female company. He knew that Mia needed to get use to her new surroundings and him being her older cousin, was obligated to help her. That's just the type of person he was.

"What are we eating today?" Mia asked while raiding Jayson's empty refrigerator. Jayson lounged on his couch as he went through the unwanted bills that found themselves in his mailbox on that particular day.

"I think Momma is cooking later." Jayson responded causing Mia's bright face to light up in anticipation of a home cooked meal. Jayson looked at her and laughed a little at her reaction.

"Stop acting like you haven't eaten in years, girl."

"I haven't, not like that," Mia exclaimed as she closed Jayson's refrigerator. Taking a seat next to Jayson, Mia let out a nostalgic sigh.

"What's wrong?" Jayson asked instinctively.

"I think something is wrong with Cam," Mia admitted causing Jayson to roll his eyes. Jayson had heard all too much about the choices Mia's naïve best friend had made and was slightly annoyed with her without even meeting her.

"Mia, I know she's your best friend, but you have to let her live. You need to be focusing on your education," Jayson lectured and Mia idly nodded. She knew that Jayson was slightly right, but she could not shake the feeling that Camryn was in a bad situation. Mia knew Gino couldn't be far from the equation.

The heart monitor slowly beeped, filling the quiet room for a short second in intervals. Camryn had been up for several minutes, but the horrible pounding in her head instilled a fear in her to open her eyes. The familiar scent of a mixture of medicines, sterilizers, and in-bound patients all blended together to form the image of a lonely hospital room. Camryn lay there, still. Fearing the worst after the events of last night came into her troubled mind. She knew that her baby was gone. There was no way it could survive that type of trauma so early on in its beautiful development.

Grief had already set in and Camryn hadn't even talked with a doctor yet. The last thing that she remembered was the heavy foot that sent a powerful blow to her chest and abdomen. She couldn't focus on how her heart burned for the demise of Twan, more so for Gino's as well.

Camryn's thoughts were interrupted by the small footsteps that traveled through the room. As she felt someone fixing the rough blanket that she was wrapped in, she slowly opened her swollen eyes and a petite Mexican woman came into view.

"Oh!" The nurse responded once she saw that Camryn had been watching her. "I must call doctor. They'll be happy to see you up."

"How long have I been unconscious?" Camryn whispered. A rough cough erupted from her throat followed by a burning sensation. Her left hand rose to it in an attempt of comfort. The nurse quickly grabbed the container of water and poured Camryn a glass.

"You have been unconscious for two and half days, Miss Lacey. Almost three."

Camryn froze at the nurse's answer to the question she was so sure she knew the answer to.

"Three days?" Camryn heaved as the pain of breathing suppressed her from saying much else. Recognizing the signs of discomfort, the nurse gently patted Camryn's now fragile leg.

"I'll go page doctor." She said while rushing out of the door.

Camryn began to panic as she realized what really happened. Twan had killed her baby and attempted to kill her, all at the mercy of Gino's lips. Her heart rate sped up as her breathing came in short breaths.

Camryn wondered if she had failed at the mission she was given. In her dream, her mom told her to protect this child with her life and she hadn't done so.

"Oh God, why?" She thought in her head. A heavy set Asian-American woman raced into the room with the nurse who was previously there on her heels.

"Miss Lacey, glad you're up, I'm Dr. Sun." She began checking Camryn's blood pressure as well as her heart rate. "Everything seems to be stable. The baby's heart rate is a little irregular but that's expected."

"The baby?" Camryn asked full of shock. "My baby is still alive?"

Dr. Sun and the nurse glanced at each other and smiled. It was very rare that a baby in the first trimester could survive such a brutal beating, but this had been one of those rare cases.

"Yes ma'am, your baby is a little fighter. The heart rate was very abnormal when you were first dropped off here at the emergency room, but when your vitals became stable, so did that baby's."

Camryn's head fell back into the pillow in pure relief. Tears of joy fell from her puffy eyes as her hands immediately flew to her mouth.

"My baby is still alive," she repeated over until it finally set in her head. At the moment, while the doctor finished running her tests, the destiny of her child had been permanently sealed into Camryn's soul. After the agony and pain of the powerful punches and brutal kicks to her womb, Gino's power could not affect this child.

Confusion lit up Camryn's face as a certain something Dr. Sun said came back into her head.

"You said I was dropped off? Who dropped me off?"

"Two young females, no relation though, they said they live across the street from you." Dr. Sun answered.

Camryn smiled as she thought about Keya and Robin. They had been running over to her house ever since they moved in some years ago. She couldn't wait to thank them for finding her.

"Miss Lacey, we're going to leave you to rest now okay? The lunch wagon should be up soon," the nurse spoke with a smile, happy to see the one that was plastered on Camryn's face.

Camryn smiled as a response. Although her body was still very weak and she knew that the obstacles were far from over, she smiled.

We go through physical pain to gain spiritual strength. Our bodies may hurt, we may bleed, but after the pain is over, we will be stronger. We gain so much more in the process. Our enemies may try to break our bodies, but they can never break our souls.

"Meka, I want pancakes!"

"No, waffles!"

Tameka sighed as Tia and Jacob sat at the kitchen table and argued over what they wanted for breakfast. It was only seven in the morning and although Tameka wasn't use to getting up that early, she knew that Tia and Jacob would be up and hungry. She had made sure they did not disturb Gino. He had come in earlier than usual last night but his whole attitude screamed "don't mess with me."

"Tia I'll make you pancakes and Jacob you can have your waffles," she said, solving the dilemma.

"Yay!" Tia and Jacob said in unison.

"Meka, is Uncle G going to eat with us?" Jacob asked and Meka sighed. Whenever Jacob referenced Gino, he got this sparkle in his eye.

"Maybe, but remember I told you not to be loud. Uncle G works very hard so he needs his rest, okay?" Tameka explained and both children nodded frantically as if they had been sent on a secret mission that only they could accomplish. Tameka smiled at their innocence before resuming her task of making breakfast.

Tameka loved spending time with Tia and Jacob. Especially after she realized that she would not be having a child of her own any time soon. Gino had made that very clear.

As if knowing that he was being discussed, Gino sluggishly walked through the entrance on the kitchen. Tia and Jacob immediately grew quiet.

"Morning, baby," Meka greeted him as she stirred the pancake batter. Gino nodded slightly as he slid his large hand over his fade.

"You two in my house and can't speak?" Gino said tickling Tia who burst into laughter.

"Hi Uncle G," both said together. Gino walked over to Meka, stood behind her and looked over her shoulder at what she was doing.

"So, I only get breakfast when the rugrats are here?" he joked but Meka didn't find it funny.

"No, you get breakfast when you're here," she said turning her head to glance at him. Gino eyed her as if to warn her against being bold before walking over to the large stainless steel refrigerator that sat up against the wall.

Meka finished her breakfast and fixed everyone's plate. She gave the kids their plates first before placing

Gino's in front of him. She also made sure they all had something to drink before sitting down in front of her own plate.

"So, do I get some of your time today?" Meka asked without looking up at her plate.

"Don't start that shit today," he quickly snapped.

"Watch your mouth in front of these kids, please," Meka whispered and Gino sighed. "I just want to spend some time with you."

"Let me take care of a few things then I'll see what I can do."

Meka would take anything she could get.

After she ate, Meka called Lori while the kids were eating to let her know she could come get them soon. She wanted to get an early start on her day. Meka planned on cleaning the house and making Gino his favorites for dinner.

She had already cleaned and dressed the kids so they helped her wash the dishes while they waited for Lori.

"I want to help wash!" Tia yelled causing Jacob to say the same thing. Meka laughed a little at how they argued over everything.

"You can take turns," Meka said. The small children smiled as they helped Meka. She could hear ESPN on the television in the living room turned up so she told the kids to quiet down a little.

The doorbell rang but no one moved.

"Meka!" Gino yelled. Meka sighed as she dried her hands on the black and white dry towel that Jacob held tightly in his hands and walked out of the kitchen and to the front door. She unlocked it, turned the knob, and smiled at her best friend.

"What's up boo, where are my babies?" Lori asked. Meka moved to let her in and closed the front door behind her. Lori's smile faded once she saw Gino seated on the couch. He rolled his eyes, knowing that it was time for him to go.

"You can speak to me, you are in my house," he stated before sliding his Jordan's onto his sock clad feet.

"Hi," Lori said plainly. Meka sighed as she asked them both to be nice. Lori sat down on the couch as Gino got up and walked towards the door.

"Call me when she's gone," he said before kissing Meka on her forehead and leaving. Meka turned and glared at Lori.

"What?" Lori asked innocently.

"Why do you always do that to him?" Meka asked as Lori grew quiet.

"I have a valid reason today," Lori said causing Meka to glance at her.

"What?" Meka asked, wondering what her best friend was getting at.

"Well, you know how that girl down the street from me works at the hospital; I think her name is Kelly?" Lori said. Meka nodded letting her know to go ahead with her story. "Well she told me some chick was dropped off by two young girls last week, some chick got beat up and Kelly read her file and it said she was pregnant."

Meka just kept on listening, not sure where Lori was going with her story.

"Well anyway, the next day she heard the girls who dropped her off talking about how they saw Twan's car across the street from where the chick lives."

"Lori, what does that have to do with Gino?" Meka asked getting impatient.

"Word on the street is Gino and his side chick haven't seen each other lately, he put a hit out on her. The way Kelly described that girl's bruises, I'm sure it was Twan's work."

Meka sighed as she tried to put together what her best friend was saying. She always knew that Gino had side chicks, but it didn't faze her because she was the one he put up in the house and claimed.

"Lori, what are you saying?" Meka asked. Lori smacked her lips in frustration, annoyed by her best friend's ignorance.

"Open your eyes, Tameka! Gino got that little girl pregnant and had Twan kill the baby."

Tameka's heartbeat stopped, as if she was going to die. Everything in her did not want to believe the harsh reality that her best friend had opened. The man she had devoted so many years to, all of her love, time and respect to, had betrayed her in the worst way possible. Tameka felt dirty, she felt disrespected and worst of all, Tameka felt cheated. If it was true that the girl was pregnant, Gino had committed the ultimate crime. How could he possibly get someone else pregnant all the while rejecting Tameka's plea for a child of her own?

"Babe, you okay?" Lori asked with concern. It wasn't as if she was trying to cause her best friend pain, but she knew that was something she had to tell her. If it would have just been a rumor on the street, Lori would have never brought it to Tameka's attention. However, the source of information happened to be a reliable one.

"Um, I need...I need to be alone." Tameka whispered. Lori frowned as she saw her best friend's world crash around her.

"Meka..." She started but Tameka quickly shook her head.

"I'm good, Lori."

Lori sighed before calling for Tia and Jacob. They said bye to Tameka and the three left. Tameka slowly sat down on the cream colored leather couch. She did not blink or move. She just sat there.

We sacrifice for the ones we love, wanting to believe that they would do the exact same for us. We hide our dissatisfaction to those around us as best as we know how. The ones who truly love us can always see through our false happiness and are always the ones to put our minds back into perspective. It takes an outside source to make us realize just how little we know.

Slow tears slid down Camryn's eyes as she saw the disappointment in her grandmother's eyes. Nana sighed as she looked at her only granddaughter and wondered how everything that was just revealed slipped through her sight.

The hospital had called Nana when Camryn was brought in. Nana wasn't as strong as she use to be, but she drove to the hospital and stayed with Camryn as long as she could. When Camryn was released, Nana demanded to know what had been going on in Camryn's life.

Camryn confessed about her relationship with Gino, which would ultimately be the disappointment that showed in Nana's face. The baby would be the only joy in this occasion. Nana had been having dreams about a child and Camryn's visions of her own mother only confirmed for Nana that the seed growing inside of Camryn had a destiny.

With the baby still being alive, as grateful as they were, the two knew that Camryn's life was still in danger. Camryn was terrified at the idea of Gino finding out that Twan had failed his mission.

"Nana, I'm so sorry," Camryn sobbed as she sat on her knees in front of her grandmother, who sat timidly on the couch. Camryn laid her head in Nana's lap.

"Stop apologizing. You have to deal with the situation now, baby," Nana said.

"But how, what am I going to do? I can't fight him," Camryn said, defeated.

"You don't have to. The battle isn't yours," Nana said making Camryn sit next to her on the couch. "Since you aren't showing yet, we'll keep this a secret. Makes those fools believe that they succeeded in the devil's work."

"What happens when I start showing?" Camryn asked curiously. Nana sighed as she gently rubbed Camryn's stomach.

"We'll deal with that when the time comes." Nana sighed right before a heavy cough fell from her lips. Camryn frowned as she quickly grabbed the glass of water on the coffee table and handed it to her.

"You need to rest, Nana," Camryn said. She felt guilty for adding stress to Nana who did not need anything else on her mind. Nana smiled at her granddaughter's concern.

"We both need to rest."

Camryn helped Nana to her room before retiring to her own. She took a long, hot shower which had been a ritual of hers for the week she had been home from the hospital and put on some cotton shorts and a long oversized tee. Camryn lay in her bed, listening to the SIRIUS Soul and R&B station on her television.

Camryn took her alone time as a thinking opportunity. She thought about how her life was before Gino and realized how good it was. She and Mia were focused on school and staying out of trouble. Her goals were still the same, but Gino had managed to push his way to the top of her priority list. She shook her head at how naïve she was. Hating the fact that it took her being knocked up and brutally beaten to realize that Gino was not what she needed.

Camryn thought of Mia and smiled at how proud she was. Her best friend was doing it big and she couldn't wait to see her again. She knew that Mia would be disappointed about the turn of events that had taken place since she left, though.

Camryn couldn't wait until her baby was born. She was sure it would be a boy. Although she was terrified to be a mother, she was warming up to the idea of it. She placed her arms lovingly around herself, mentally asking God to hold her as well.

"My baby."

Tameka was still seeing red as Gino arrived home that evening. She had changed from her normal attire into some red sweat pants that were rolled up her calf muscles and a black tank top, showing off the cross that decorated her left shoulder with her mom's name written in the middle. She stood at the stove cooking. It was slightly therapeutic to her. It calmed her in a way because she felt she was actually doing something with her life.

She sighed before stopping to pull her hair into a sloppy bun, revealing the cursive letters on the right side of her neck that silently spoke her name.

Tameka's cell phone rang again as Lori called her for the third time and once again, Tameka pressed ignore.

She didn't want to hear Lori tell her how she needed to leave Gino alone and that he's no good. Tameka honestly did not want to hear that at all. Gino was, as pathetic as it seemed, the only thing that Tameka knew. Gino had taken care of her for the last seven years. What was she supposed to do without him?

Her heart sped up as the alarm beeped and the back door opened. She kept on cooking in an attempt to surpass a dry conversation.

Gino strolled into the kitchen with a look on his face that on any particular day would have melted Tameka's ice feelings. He slid his muscular arms around Meka's waist and roughly kissed the back of her neck.

"My woman got it smelling good in here," he semi-yelled to no one in particular. Tameka's leg began to shake as she struggled to hold her tongue. She wanted to scream and show her pain but her past experiences with Gino advised her to do otherwise.

"Why didn't you call me when motor mouth left?"

"I didn't want to disturb you. I figured that you would be busy."

"Not too busy for you," he answered. Tameka stopped stirring the macaroni noodles and looked up at the empty wall. Her heart began to hurt even more as she realized that Lori's admission was inevitably true. Gino was only sweet to Tameka when he felt guilty about something.

"Are you in for the night?" Tameka asked as she drained the noodles and checked on the steak in the oven. Gino sat down at one of the dining table chairs and relaxed.

"Yeah, Twan is handling things. I need to rest," he responded.

Tameka nodded in response as she continued to cook. Gino made a few business calls at the dining room table before heading out. Tameka could hear his footsteps treading up the hard wood floor steps.

Tameka's heart beat sped up as she struggled to breath. She stepped back from the stove, pressed her backside against the opposite counter and placed her on hand over her heart. She wanted to cry about the place she was in right now.

It was like a bad Lifetime movie and Tameka wanted to get out of it. She hadn't even seen the girl and already she was plotting on how to get rid of her. Deep down in her heart she knew that she should have been plotting on how to leave Gino, but realistically that wasn't going to happen.

After Tameka's initial pain was gone, anger flooded in on the next tide. Tameka had been talking about having a baby for several months to no avail, how could some other girl be pregnant by the one she was devoted to? That didn't make any sense to her at all. She had tried so hard to maintain her cool and show Gino that she wasn't focused on his side conquests but it hurt. Tameka was honestly hurting inside; the pain was something that had built up and she had tried her best not to let out. The pressure of denial erupted in her like a shaken up Pepsi and popped the top. She was pissed, no Tameka was furious.

As Gino's footsteps ascended back down the steps, Tameka quickly got herself together and pulled out the steaks she had broiling. Gino smiled as the food came into view and rubbed his chiseled abdomen. Tameka quietly made his plate before making hers. Instead of sitting down at the table with him, she wrapped her plate up and put it in the refrigerator. She had suddenly lost her appetite. Gino looked up from his meal and raised an eyebrow.

"Babe, what you doing?" Gino asked as Tameka opted for a vodka bottle and a small shot glass. She took her first shot before answering.

"I'm not hungry," she answered before taking another shot. Gino watched her for a few seconds before shaking his head and turning back to his plate.

"You need to slow down on them shots," he advised. Tameka waited until he looked at her again to take another. "Alright, I won't be picking your ass up off the floor in a few." He joked, but Tameka didn't laugh. Gino slid his fork on the table and turned towards his woman. He sighed before leaning back in the chair and to the side, resting his right arm on his thigh. He licked his lips before motioning for Tameka. She obediently walked over to him and was pulled down onto his lap. As much as her mind wanted to protest and throw a fit, she didn't move.

Gino removed the bottle that seemed to be glued into Tameka's hand and placed it next to his plate. He then wrapped his arms around her and pulled her further up on his lap. Tameka looked off at the opposite wall. A tear slid unconsciously down Tameka's eye before she realized it.

"What's this for?" Gino asked wiping it away. Tameka just shrugged her shoulders, not having the energy to deal with the argument that would result from what she wanted to say. Gino didn't question her motive, he really wasn't that concerned.

Tameka snatched the bottle back and drank straight from it. The vodka burned a trail down her throat and warmed her insides.

"You want to go out? I have to head downtown later. We can hit up The Lounge afterwards." Gino offered. Tameka smirked at the game that he was playing. Gino was very persistent in keeping his personal business off of the streets, but if there was ever a time where he thought something would catch up with him, he played his best hand. Tameka expected to go out, go shopping, get treated as the queen Gino claimed she was, for the next few days, maybe even weeks. She would play it out and take what she was giving for now. Her current beef did not lie with Gino, this time.

Tameka slid off of her man's lap with a slightly new attitude.

"Let me go get ready."

Isn't it just like an ignorant female, to fault the next one for the same thing? You attract, you love, you sacrifice and you hurt, but never put the blame on the one that causes all of those emotions – yourself. We look to the one we love and we look to the one they lust after, we never look to ourselves. This, 90% of the time if not 100% of the time, always ends in despair.

"Long time, no hear," Mia beamed into the phone after her best friend's voice became audible.

"Hey babe, I miss you," Camryn spoke as soon as she heard Mia's voice. Camryn asked Mia how she had been right before stuffing a forkful of chicken Alfredo in her mouth. Nana had woken up feeling good and decided to cook. Camryn wasn't complaining. It had been almost a month since both of their hospital stays and Camryn was finally showing. That meant she was to stay out of the public eye as much as possible. She went to work and came home.

"I'm good, ready for this semester to be over with though," Mia responded.

"Well, you're half way through it."

"I'm still not use to it," Mia admitted about college life. "You know I'm not used to actually studying."

"You'll get over it," Camryn joked. A small laugh sounded from Mia's end of the phone as they caught up on the past few months.

"I talked to your mom the other day," Camryn confessed.

"Did you? She didn't even tell me."

"Yeah, she called me and cussed me out about being her other child and not coming to see her since you've been gone," Camryn said with a smile on her face, remembering the quick conversation.

"You know how she is," Mia said.

"I know, things have just been hectic over here," Camryn sighed as she looked down at her pregnant belly, slightly smiling.

"I hope it doesn't have anything to do with Gino," Mia stated boldly. Camryn smirked knowing that statement was due to appear in their telephone reunion.

"You know what Mia, for once it doesn't, it's about me this time."

"Aw, does that mean what I hope it means?"

"Yes it does, I am officially done being Gino's toy," Camryn said, proudly.

"Cam, I am so glad to hear that," Mia confessed. "I had been worried about what he's been doing to you since I've been gone. I expected the worst but I'm so glad that you shook that nasty habit. When I get home we're celebrating." Mia went on and Camryn produced a fake laugh.

Yes, it was true that she had shaken her addiction to the Gino that had revealed itself in the event of her pregnancy but she wasn't sure if her addiction to the Gino she grew to love was kicked.

Maybe it was the fact that his seed was embedded into her womb or the fact that she had been so naive to his empty promises for so long, but Camryn knew that it couldn't be so easy to leave him. She felt that as soon as Gino switched his role back to the sweet, smooth talker she was hypnotized by, it was bye bye for her new found independence.

She tried to convince herself that the horrid things he had put her through in the last few months was enough to build a hatred for him in her heart, but the truth was that it wasn't.

"Cam, how's Nana?" Mia asked after her rant about the terrible ways of Gino.

"She's better," Camryn said smiling at the more jovial subject. "She makes me nervous with all the moving around she's doing but she's a lot better."

"That's what's up!" Mia exclaimed causing Camryn to laugh once again. She hadn't laughed this much in months. Although she realized just how much she missed being in Mia's presence, it felt good to talk to her.

"Yeah, that's what I said."

"Hey, we have a three day weekend in two weeks, I'm thinking of coming home."

Camryn's heart skipped a beat at the thought of having to tell Mia about the baby. She wasn't sure if she wanted to tell her over the phone, but when she saw her she would have no choice.

"I really just wanted to stay up here because Ma is tripping, but I want to see you so…"

"How about I come up there?" Camryn blurted out as the idea came in her head. She had been hiding from Gino and his goons and she needed a getaway.

"Really? That would be hot, you can catch the train so you don't have to drive. It's only like $26 dollars for round trip," Mia said with excitement.

"Yeah, I'll do that. Nana is trying to get me to go to her sister's place with her and I didn't want to go so I can just come see you that weekend," Camryn said, both nervous and excited.

"Great, but I have to go. I'll call you later?" Mia asked.

"Yeah, I'll be home."

"Alright, bye."

"Bye, babe."

After the call disconnected, Camryn sighed as she thought about Mia's reaction to the pregnancy. Camryn figured Mia would probably say 'I told you so' once she explained to her everything that had happened since her child was conceived.

Nana walked into the living room all smiles. Camryn smiled at her happiness before asking her where she had been.

"Out with a friend, nosy." Nana answered. Camryn perched her lips in a playful yet sarcastic manner.

"Well, excuse me!"

"Child hush," Nana said laughing before pulling some money out of her purse. "This is for you."

"What is this for Nana?" Camryn asked taking it from her, bawling her left fist around it.

"I won some money at bingo and since you've been spending yours to help with the bills, I decided to break you off." Camryn laughed at her choice of words.

"Nana, you don't have to give me any money." Camryn said trying to give it back to her. Nana swatted her hand away and shook her head.

"Go buy you something nice, there are some good sales at the mall." Nana announced and Camryn's face lit up at the mention of the mall.   She soon frowned as she realized it was a Friday afternoon, the mall would be packed.

"But I'm supposed to stay in the house."

"The mall is just down the street, we can go together." Nana said letting Camryn know it would be okay. Camryn smiled and agreed to go.

Nana waited for Camryn to get ready and they headed to Viewpoint Mall. Camryn was so excited to get out of the house that she wasn't sure which store she wanted to go in. Nana caught sight of a maternity store and pulled Camryn towards it.

"These clothes look like they are for people in their last days of pregnancy," Camryn complained.

"They'll have things in your size. You can get some nice dresses for church. Oh, look at those adorable shirts."

Camryn watched Nana fuss over the clothes and realized how excited she was to be a great-grandmother.

The pure, untainted gleam in her eye told it all. Camryn wondered why she hadn't noticed it before but it actually made her feel better about being a mother.

"Oh, I do like this dress, Nana." Camryn admitted while looking at a red sundress with yellow designs. She found her size and removed it from the rack.

"You need to get a bigger size," Nana commanded as Camryn held the dress up to herself.

"You're right, this one will be tight," Camryn said deciding to go up two sizes, she opted for 8.

"You're not going to be one of those weight-obsessed pregnant women are you?" Nana joked. Camryn violently shook her head with a smile on her face.

"I like my thickness," Camryn boasted, looking at herself in the mirror. Nana laughed before walking over to another rack with sleeveless shirts on them. Camryn was still very petite but the weight she had gained so far was fine with her. Her lips were a thicker, which she loved; her breasts were fuller, which she loved; but the thing she loved the most was her hips were spreading, she always disliked the fact that she had no hips, even though her butt was a nice size. Her new hips just made her shape look better to her.

After Nana picked out a few shirts and another dress and Camryn picked out some long tunics and leggings, they decided they had had enough of the maternity store. As they walked through the mall, they came across a woman giving puppies away in front of the pet store. Nana was ecstatic in the fact that the woman was giving away Yorkshire puppies but Camryn was skeptically. Those puppies usually sold for $300 or more.

"What's wrong with them?" Camryn asked causing the woman to sigh.

"It's me with the problem. I have two in an apartment that I am not allowed to have pets in. A litter of puppies will increase my chances of getting caught. I can't take care of seven puppies," the woman confessed in desperation.

"Are they certified?" Camryn asked as Nana consumed herself with playing with a light brown one.

"Yes, and I have the papers. All I need from you is your word that you will take care of it."

"I'll take it," Nana announced, "But you must let me give you something for it."

"No ma'am that is not necessary." the woman said handing Nana the papers for that particular dog.

Nana ended up buying some things for the puppy in the store while Camryn held him.

"Nana, you aren't even going to take care of this dog."

"You will," she said with a smile. Camryn rolled her eyes before looking down at the dog. He was kind of cute.

"What are we going to name him?" Camryn asked as they walked towards the entrance of the mall.

"I'll think of something."

"G, come on we won't be in here long."

"I don't want to be here longer than ten minutes, Meka."

Camryn froze as she heard the voice she dreaded every night in her nightmares.

Hearing his voice after so long had instantly put fear in her. She didn't know what to do. Nana noticed it and assumed what had happened. She gently grabbed Camryn's arm and proceeded to the exit. Camryn placed the puppy up to the side of her face in an attempt to hide herself. Before she did this, she spotted a glimpse of Tameka, who was preoccupied with Gino's stubbornness. Camryn's face felt hot and as soon as she was safely in the car she admitted her frustration.

"He lied to me!" she yelled at no one in particular. Nana observed her granddaughter's actions as hot tears slid down Camryn's face. "Nana all this time he told me he wasn't with her anymore. How could I have been so stupid?"

"Baby, we all get stupid when love is involved. You shouldn't be so hard on yourself." Nana said with a hard exterior. On the inside she was crying as well. It pained her terribly to see her only grandchild go through these things. With her mom not being here, Nana felt partially to blame for never warning Camryn about guys like Gino.

"All this time," Camryn repeated as it finally set in how much a fool for Gino he was. All the times he falsely admitted to Camryn that Tameka was still stuck on him, she actually had a reason to be. Camryn did not believe how naïve she had been. Gino never attempted to invite her over. Camryn was so bent on being his woman that she didn't realize the reason she wasn't was because he still had one.

She tried to start the car but Nana took the keys.

"Get yourself together first," Nana demanded, handing her a soft tissue. Camryn obediently shook her head before sitting back in the driver's seat.

This was a reality check. An earlier admittance of harbored feelings had driven this discovery to light. It is a hard thing to admit that you were in love with the wrong one, but an even harder one is realizing you were the other woman when you thought you were the only. Being naïve is not a virtue, only until you found out the truth do you realize that being in the dark is lonely. Fortunately, this discovery and this admittance create an even stronger separation between you and your pain. Your pain no longer is desirable to you, which means; mentally, you're free.

When the two arrived home, Keya and Robin were on their porch patiently waiting for Camryn's arrival. Camryn smiled once she saw them and handed the puppy to Nana. She waited until Nana was in the house to speak.

"Hey, you two," Camryn greeted them.

"Hey," Robin said nervously as Keya just stared at Camryn.

"Are you okay?" she finally asked. Camryn smiled as she nodded her head.

"I never got to thank you two for find…"

"Don't worry about it," Keya said cutting Camryn off. Camryn nodded before slightly stretching, causing the shirt she was wearing to ride up a little. Robin and Keya both gasped at the sight of her belly.

"The baby made it?" Keya asked. Camryn nodded proudly.

"Thanks to you."

The two young girls smiled as their good deed brought reason to their current punishment of sneaking out of the house in the first place. Knowing that they had saved two lives made their temporary house arrest insignificant.

"We're so glad you're okay. When we saw you lying there we were horrified," Keya admitted. Camryn sighed as she thought about that terrible night.

"I was too, I can't believe how blessed I was that you two found me in time. You know, I was thinking if I have a girl, I might let you guys name her," Camryn announced.

"Aw!" they both said, causing all three of them to laugh. Their laughter subsided after their mother screamed their names from across the street.

"We have to go," Robin said as they both stood up from the cushioned bench.

"Come by anytime," Camryn invited as they both said bye and ran across the street.

Twan strolled down the sidewalk, gliding past those who scattered at the sight of him. His thick 18k gold chain swung as he stepped, slightly swaying side to side as he made his way through the neighborhood. He smirked knowing that fear lay in the hearts of those who saw him because it slightly amused him. To him, his influence in the streets was his air; Twan lived to instill fear.

The boom of an expensive sound system filled Twan's ears as he knew his lifelong friend was close by. Twan huffed. Gino had been an irritating itch ever since Twan handled that business for him. That let him know that Gino wasn't so sure about leaving Camryn alone. Twan would not say anything because he wanted to see the situation play itself out.

The clean, black Lincoln truck pulled into the empty parking lot of an abandoned gas station, causing Twan to walk towards it. Gino stepped smoothly out of the driver's side, leaving the door open, allowing the whole block to hear Rick Ross proclaiming his status. Leaning against the truck, he nodded towards his comrade.

"How's business?" Gino asked.

"Business," Twan ritually answered causing Gino to smirk. Twan had been using that term as a synonym for good ever since they started building their empire years back. Gino was the mastermind with the means while Twan was the muscle.

"Just like music," Gino said in somewhat relief. All week he had been busy spending away Tameka's suspicious and he was exhausted. He knew Tameka liked to shop but this week had been ridiculous. Gino figured word had gotten back to her about Camryn. He was sure that she would speak on it, but she hadn't.

"Ay, that little cat Afton is trying to get put on." Twan informed Gino, who inquisitively looked at him.

"You vouch for him?"

"Hell no, but he's been coming up on the block every morning giving word to Darius to get word to us," Twan said.

Gino nodded his head but did not respond. He was not sure if adding to his camp was the best thing to do at the moment. Although he was close to eliminating his problem, he still wasn't exactly sure who his snake was. He couldn't lie and say that another hand on his Manchester block wouldn't help.

"We can put him down on Chester and see how it works. Make Jay shadow his ass until he's up to par," Twan said, reading Gino's mind.

"We'll see," Gino said sliding off his Marc Jacob sunglasses and quickly licking his lips, "Ay, when you did that for me, did anybody see you?" Gino asked. Twan frowned, wondering what Gino was referring to but smirked when he realized he was talking about Camryn.

"It was dark, nobody was out," Twan stated simply. Gino looked at him for a while before nodding. "Tameka got word?"

"She ain't saying it, but I think that rat she run with told her something." Gino responded.

"How would she know?" Twan asked.

"Lori's nosy ass knows everything."

Twan nodded as to say he knew. He himself had once tried to get with Lori, even though Chase was one of Gino's generals. Twan wasn't the most loyal person and Lori was not having it. She went off on him about him and Gino's ways so much that Twan eventually lost interest. He didn't dwell on that.

Gino looked at Twan and wondered why he never really seen him with any females. There were lots of girls that showed interest in Twan, but Gino rarely saw him take them up on their offers.

He glanced around one of his many blocks and noticed that the women were out and showing everything on that particular day. Gino saw a familiar face and remembered something from a few days ago.

"Ay, you know that chick they call Baby?" Gino asked Twan, who raised an eyebrow at the mention of the name.

"The tall, chocolate cutie?" Twan asked and Gino nodded with a smile. "What about her?"

"She came up on me a few days ago and was damn near drooling while talking about you. Told me as soon as I saw you to let you know she's ready!"

"She's ready?" Twan asked somewhat interested. Gino laughed at the reaction.

"That's what she said, Baby want you." Gino said and Twan nodded as his mind switched from work to Baby.

"I might have to get at her," Twan said more to himself than to Gino. Gino kept nodding, happy that Twan was taking an interest in something other than work. Gino was about his business but work had to be downsized with a little play.

A week and a half had gone by and Tameka was finally delivered the news she had waited for. Lori was able to find out where the girl worked at and when she would be there. Tameka had no doubt that Lori would do it because she had been doing that type of undercover work since they were younger.

Tameka wasn't sure what she planned to do once she saw the girl, who Lori informed was named Camryn. Part of her just wanted to see her; Tameka wanted to see the one who had carried the seed of her man, even if that time was short lived. Although Tameka wasn't very sure of what she would do, but she knew that she had to see Camryn for herself.

"So you want me to come get you?" Lori asked through the receiver as Tameka looked at her own reflection in the mirror.

"I have to see her," Tameka said answering Lori's question. Lori let out a sympathetic sigh as she informed Tameka to be ready in 20 minutes. Tameka looked quickly through her dresser to find something to wear. She quickly found herself debating over the simplest thing; sweats or jeans, fitted tee or beater, sneakers or sandals.

"What am I doing?" Tameka asked herself aloud as she pulled out a pair of dark red sweats, a white fitted tee with red stars on it and some white ankle socks. Tameka quickly slid on her outfit of choice, careful not to mess up the wrap in her hair, before pulling her red and white Air Jordan Fushions from under her and Gino's bed.

While Tameka was making sure her hair was still intact, Lori was honking her horn. Tameka quickly grabbed her Chanel shades and purse before walking out of the room.

When Tameka got into Lori's car, an old 2pac track filled her ears. It didn't surprise her because that was all Lori listened to. She even had Tia and Jacob singing 2pac on occasion. Tameka inhaled the scent that came off of the tightly rolled joint sticking out of the corner of Lori's mouth.

"I would have been here sooner but I had to drop the twins off at Chase's mom's," Lori explained as she pulled out of the long driveway. Tameka nodded, not in the least bit worried about why Lori was a little later than expected.

"Are you sure you got some concrete information," Tameka asked. Lori smacked her lips, somewhat offended.

"Shut up and ride."

It took about 15 minutes for Lori to get to their destination. She reversed into a parking space so that her car was facing the entrance to Wireless Communications. Tameka's leg began to shake as she watched the door closely.

"You know who she is right?" Tameka asked.

"Meka quit tripping. I'll tell you when she comes out the door." Lori said assuring Tameka that she knew what she was doing. Tameka sighed in anticipation. Every time the door opened, Tameka's heart dropped, wondering if the face she was seeing was the woman who had been lying up with her beloved. If the face she was seeing was the woman her man had impregnated. Tameka's rage grew with her anticipated.

Suddenly, the door opened and a smile so bright caught Tameka's attention. The short caramel tone girl that stepped out had to be Camryn. The bright red highlights that led up into a dark brown ponytail reminded Tameka of a style she used to rock. Her nose flared as she had to admit to herself that the woman she was staring at was descent. She would later admit that she honestly felt threatened by her, knowing what Gino's usual type was.

"That's her," Lori said looking up from her joint, confirming what Tameka already felt. Her heart rate beat faster as she began to see red, wanting to murder her man's other woman where she stood. Tameka quickly reached for the door but Lori held her back.

"Don't be dumb, Meka," Lori stated plainly. Tameka fumed as she looked at her best friend.

"Don't be dumb, Meka? Lori, I've been dumb for seven damn years!" Tameka said as tears ran down her face. "I've been with this man for years, lying up with him when he wants, cooking, cleaning his damn house every day, playing the good little wifey while he gets her pregnant?" Tameka said thrusting her finger towards Camryn, who was talking to someone as she walked towards her car. "How could he do this to me? How I could I let him do this to me?"

Lori looked at her best friend before putting her joint into the ash tray.

"Look, Tameka I understand you're upset, but beating this girl up in front of her job, only a few weeks after she got out of the hospital from having a miscarriage is not a good look for you. Whatever you want to do about this situation, we need to plan this out."

Tameka nodding, knowing that Lori was absolutely right and that she had to be smart about the situation. Tameka eye's followed Camryn all the way to her car.

"Follow her so I can see where she lives."

Camryn sat comfortably on the cushioned porch swing with Nana's new puppy sleeping on her lap. Nana had decided to name him King. Camryn wasn't feeling that too much but she figured that she would get use to it. She gently rubbed his neck as he rested next to her unborn child.

She had been thinking about her baby a lot. It surprised her that she hadn't

dwelled on seeing Gino with Tameka. Now that she thought back on her wasted time as Gino's conquest, she can't figure out how she didn't know he was still with Tameka. Camryn would shake her head at her own naivety but also wondered if Tameka was as blind as she. She quickly dismissed the thought as her mind switched back to her child.

Camryn ultimately wanted her baby to be healthy, but she also desperately wished it was a little girl. Although her mother's spirit had already revealed to her that she would bare a son, Camryn couldn't help but wonder what her little girl would be like. She could remember things her mother did so clearly even several years after her demise. She wanted to do those things with her own daughter. Camryn wasn't sure if she could raise a man. She felt the only thing she could teach him was how to treat a woman but would that be enough? Never knowing if her child's father would eventually accept him was a slight heartache for Camryn.

In any case, Camryn knew that her baby would be okay. She also knew that Twan's fist wouldn't be the last of Gino's antics. She wouldn't be able to hide the fact that she was still pregnant for long.

Main Street was particularly busy on that day. Camryn had noticed several cars riding past that weren't regulars on the street but charged it to the weekend. While she was sitting on the porch texting Mia she noticed a black two-door Cobalt ride by several times. She didn't think anything of it at first until she noticed that it would slightly slow down but speed up once it passed her house. She sighed as she realized it had to be someone in Gino's company. Camryn pulled on her oversized tee shirt to make sure that her pregnant belly was not visible.

Not even five minutes later, the car was back on her street, only a few houses down from her. Camryn's heart rate increased as the car pulled over in front of her house. The passenger door opened and soon Tameka appeared getting out of it. Camryn sat still, not sure as to what to do or how Tameka found out who she was and where she lived. As Tameka slowly walked up her brick path, Camryn knew that she couldn't worry about that right now.

"Can I help you?" Camryn asked in the softest voice possible. Tameka slid her dark brown Chanel sunglasses off of her face and frowned.

"Are you Camryn?"

The question was so simple but Camryn pondered lying. She figured that Tameka already knew who she was and that a yes would only confirm it. If she lied and said that she wasn't Camryn it would only make the situation worse.

"Yes, I'm Camryn," She stated boldly. When those words left her lips, Tameka looked her up and down before smirking.

"I'm sure you know who I am." Tameka stated arrogantly.

"Should I?" Camryn stated causing Tameka to frown.

"Yea you should, you were sleeping with my man, don't play dumb!"

Tameka shouted and although her insides were shaking, Camryn stayed calm. Nana always taught her not to let people see her weakness.

"Who is your man?" Camryn asked. She could tell that Tameka was getting upset.

"I'm not about to play games with you, we are way past games," Tameka exclaimed and Camryn sighed, because she was right.

"You're right," Camryn answered, "But I wasn't just sleeping with him and at the time and I was told that you were out of the picture."

"Bullshit!"

"Believe what you want, but obviously we both got played," Camryn said.

"I didn't get played sweetie, you did," Tameka said with a phony smile. Camryn looked at her and smirked, wondering why she was trying so hard to prove a lie.

"Alright," Camryn stated plainly. Before Tameka could respond, the screen door creaked and Nana stepped out onto the porch. She looked directly at Tameka and smiled.

"Hey baby," Nana said looking Tameka up and down. Tameka bit her lip before looking back towards the car she came in.

"Hi ma'am, how you doing?" Tameka said in a respectable manner.

"I'm fine," Nana said before turning to Camryn, "Can you help me with dinner?" she asked. Camryn looked to Tameka before nodding.

"Yes ma'am," Camryn said while wrapping King up in her arms and standing up, carefully not to show her belly. Tameka waited until Nana was in the house to stop Camryn.

"This isn't over," Tameka warned her. Camryn sighed, tired of Gino's drama.

"I'm sure it isn't."

We do so many crazy things for love. We can make the dumbest mistakes because we thought love was there. Females, in particular, seem to be the butt of jokes when it comes to the crazy things they do for love. We blame everyone else is to blame for our failed relationships but never look at the part we played in it ourselves. But, love is a beautiful thing, isn't it?

A Man Child would be born

Talk of a big party being thrown buzzed through the streets as Gino's workers made their rounds. A few to each block was Gino's strategic placing, no less than two but no more than four was the advice Twan had given him some years ago when his camp began to grow. Back then Gino only ran a block given to him by an older cat. Gino still had milk on his breath when the demise of the one who ran the neighborhood before him came to pass.

Twan smirked as he remembered the stressful days he spent helping Gino raise his dynasty. He had to admit that they had put in work and made something out of little to nothing. Gino would often talk of getting out of the game in years to come, but Twan would always wave him off, letting him know that he was born, bred, and would die hustling. He was the epitome of the streets.

Twan sat with a few on his concrete porch a few feet away from one of their selling spots. Unlike Gino, who had relocated to the other side of town and put Tameka up in a town house, Twan stayed in the middle of commerce. He had several reasons for this but the ultimate one was he felt comfortable where he was. It was his home and he knew how home ran.

"So what it look like?" Twan asked the young cat sitting next to him who had his eye on a few girls across the street. His smooth caramel face smirked at the antics of them as they made every attempt to be noticed. His wandering brown eyes told them they had succeeded, slightly. Twan smirked at the youth knowing those girls saw an up and coming hustler and the young cat saw open legs. "Jay stop drooling and get on this business," Twan joked. The porch lit up with laughter as Jay ran his small hand down the length of his fade.

"Dawg, I can't call it," Jay admitted. Twan raised an eyebrow at his response.

"If you don't need him, let me know," Twan spat causing Jay to sigh in frustration.

"I'm saying, we can use an extra body but training that little dude?" Jay said glancing at Twan sideways. "All my sources say he's hardheaded. I'm not trying to hold his hand and feed him while its money to be made."

Twan could do nothing but respect the knowledge Jay just dropped, almost as if it had fallen from his own lips.

"That's what I like about you, young cat," Twan said passing Jay the blunt he had been protecting. Jay smirked at his sign of approval. "Fact still lies that with this rat around we're losing money," Twan said making sure to hold the eye of every party sitting on his steps. "We need another body."

Jay nodded his head but perched his lips, letting his comrades know he wasn't feeling the plan too much. Twan could tell that putting Afton down on Chester may be a problem if he wasn't ready. Half of them wondered why Afton wouldn't start on a slow corner instead of a busier one.

"Tell G to put Case up on Manchester with Jay and put Afton down on State. Feel the little dude out," Baywood, one of the few that started out with Twan and Gino spook. Twan nodded to the beat of an old Jigga track while mulling it over.

"That could work."

The thought of work faded away from their minds as a vision of slight perfection came into view. It was as if the three girls who had turned the corner on the sidewalk were gliding in slow motion, like in the movies. A variety of caramel hues glistened from exposed limbs in tight, short clothes. Jay, Baywood, and Twan followed the path of legs up curvy hips and full breasts to see who they had been gawking at. Twan found himself smirking at the sight of Baby, who was walking in the middle looking fine as the day. She was wearing a green body suit that looked more like a swimsuit than a shirt and some dark denim shorts that happened to be unbuttoned. Twan even smirked at her small feet being decorated with white and green Jordans. The same smile he fought off was one that she was throwing back at him. She even added a lip lick before she stopped in front of Twan's mailbox.

"You see me?" Baby asked, posing up against Twan's mailbox as if they were photographers at a photo shoot. Twan nodded at her in response, which caused a smile to spread across her face, showcasing her dimples. Twan knew she was bad, but he had never been this close to her. Bad wasn't the word for Baby.

Everyone around was watching her, anticipating her move. Twan even found himself wondering what slick comment would come out of her mouth, as her reputation preceded her. He remained calm because he knew why she wanted him. He wasn't stalking her like the dudes sitting on his porch with him.

"I know you see me," Baby reiterated with a smile on her face.

"You heard about the party?" Jay asked trying to get some of her attention.

"Are y'all coming?" One of the girls with Baby asked.

"We don't do parties, it will probably be lame anyway," Baywood said. Baby frowned.

"I don't do lame, boo," she said. Twan's interest in the party suddenly sparked.

"It's at your spot?" Jay asked and Baby nodding while her attention stayed on Twan.

"You are coming right?" She asked turning slightly to the side and licking her lips once again.

"You sure you ready for me?" Twan asked cutting straight to the chase. Her girls mumbled something as Jay and Baywood watched the exchange. Baby bit her bottom lip and gave Twan a look that answered his question all on it's on. Just in case it didn't, she replied.

"Try me."

Camryn frowned as the sonance of violent coughs erupted from Nana's bedroom. Camryn cringed at the image of mucus caught in Nana's throat and hurried to finish her soup. Camryn tried not to shed a tear as the coughing continued. She should be used to the bad days by now.

"Nana, I'm almost done do you want something to drink?" Camryn yelled not actually expecting an answer. She turned the stove down to low before pouring cool water into a tall glass. With her left hand on her unruly unborn child's covering and the other clutching the glass, Camryn made her way into Nana's bedroom.

"Here, drink this," Camryn demanded as she sat next to Nana on her small bed. Camryn hated the bed and always tried to buy Nana a bigger one but she always rejected the offer.

"The soup is almost done," Camryn stated blankly, sadness filling her eyes as she watched her Nana.

"Child, I heard you the first time you said it," Nana stated with annoyance. "Shouldn't you be getting ready to leave?"

"Nana, I'm not leaving you alone like this!" Camryn stated. She looked at her grandmother wondering why she thought that she would.

"Camryn, I can take care of myself for a two days and besides Mia is expecting you," Nana said trying to convince her to leave. Camryn shook her head as she grabbed the house phone and dialed Mia's number.

Mia picked up on the first ring.

"Hey Cam," she greeted in a jovial manner.

"Hey Mia, what's up?" Camryn asked in a hurry.

"Nothing, cleaning up for you," Mia announced causing Camryn to smile weakly. "What time are you heading out?"

"Babe, I'm not going to be able to make it. Nana isn't feeling too good and I'm not sure I want to leave her."

"Oh," Mia said in a dry tone. Camryn wanted to cry because she needed to see Mia and explain everything to her. She didn't know what to do at that moment. "Well I guess I can drive home today."

"Really?" Camryn asked in shock. Mia laughed at her tone.

"Yes, my cousin wants to see Momma anyway so I can just ride down with him."

"Oh, I'm so glad I still get to see you!" Camryn squealed in excitement.

"Me too, we should be there around seven or so."

"Okay, I'll be home."

Camryn took a second to smile after hanging up with her best friend before getting up to get Nana's soup.

Camryn was so excited to see Mia. It had been close to four months and Camryn had been through so much without her. She couldn't believe that in a course of four months she would be detached from her love and her town. Camryn was certain that Mia would declare her dumb and say plenty of 'I told you so's' but Camryn knew she would be there for her in the end because that was what best friends did.

Camryn pulled a black soup bowl from its holding place in the cabinet and put it down next to the stove. She grabbed a pot holder and slid it around the warm handle, tipped it over and carefully watched as the hot contents cascaded into the bowl. After hearing Nana cough once again, Camryn pulled a silver spoon out of the dish holder and quickly made her way back to Nana's room.

An hour later, Nana was taking her nap and Camryn found herself cleaning the house. She was never one to clean but it seemed to be the only thing that calmed her lately. After cleaning her bedroom, her and Nana's separate bathrooms and the kitchen, Camryn made a beeline to the living room.

Every so often, she would look down at her stomach and smile.

After cleaning the house, Camryn decided to clean herself and drew some hot bath water. As she relaxed with her head up against the shower wall, horrid thoughts of what would happen when Gino, Tameka, and Twan found out that their plan to terminate her pregnancy failed clouded her mind. She could feel a thunderstorm in the works but the severity of it was beyond her.

Camryn slightly tilted her head to the left as her right big toe gently tapped against the round silver knob under the faucet. In her mind, she could almost count the times that her and her ex-lover had soaked in that very tub, enjoying each other. It had been in that same tub that Gino held Camryn against him protectively, claiming her as his. It had been in that very tub that Camryn confessed her love to Gino. Camryn kicked at the silver knob in frustration. She was very disappointed in her own naivety. She had been involved with Gino since she was 17 and with her 20th birthday just a week away, Camryn felt that three years was too long to be somebody's fool.

Her slender arms wrapped protectively around her midsection, marveling in the fact that another life was present in her being. There had been placed, by God, an unconditional bond within her and it brightened her days to know that. Camryn was very excited about her birthday, as it would be the day she found out the sex of her baby. The night her mother came to her in a dream was steadfast in Camryn's mind as the day drew closer. If she was indeed carrying Gino's son, Camryn would have an even deeper confirmation of the things foreseen.

"He would be something special," Camryn mumbled.

As the light skin on her fingertips began to wrinkle, Camryn exited her aquatic sanction. She took her time motorizing her body and applied cocoa butter to her stomach. Deciding on looking somewhat decent, Camryn pulled out a long, light blue sleeveless tunic and a pair of white leggings with light blue polka dots. Satisfied with her attire, Camryn brushed her hair into a bun and placed a thin, light blue headband over her freshly cut Chinese bangs.

"I should take a picture," she giggled at her own goofiness before glancing at her cell phone and smiling. Mia would be there any minute.

Camryn walked out of her room and down the hall to Nana's. When she walked in, Nana was up and watching her soap operas. Feeling another presence in her room, Nana turned and smiled at Camryn.

"Well, don't you clean up nice," Nana joked causing Camryn to smile. "Are you and Mia going out?"

"No," Camryn replied, "I do need to go pick up my prescription but I'm not sure how she'll take the pregnancy," Camryn admitted. Nana nodded, understanding wholeheartedly.

"I'm sure she'll be excited to be a Godmother," Nana assured her. Camryn had come to swallow two large pills since her hospitalization: Nana wasn't going to be around forever and when the news of her still being pregnant got out, she might not be around too much longer either. Mia was the only one she could trust with her child.

Camryn stood at the window as an unfamiliar car pulled up with the company she was expecting. She peeked out from behind the maroon sheer curtains and smiled at the sight of her best friend.

"That must be her cousin's car," Camryn answered her own question as she watched Mia walk up the sidewalk. She inhaled deeply as she prepared for her best friend's reaction that was sure to come as soon as Camryn opened the door. For some reason, in that instant, Camryn was more afraid of Mia finding out than Gino. She began to hyperventilate as the doorbell rang, her feet carrying her towards it.

Camryn took a deep breath before opening the door. "Hey baby…Camryn!"

Mia's face had gone from excited to confusion as she saw her pregnant best friend. Camryn instantly began to cry at Mia's reaction.

An hour later, Mia sat on the couch staring blankly at the wall as Camryn watched her. Camryn had just explained to Mia what had been happening since the day she left and Mia was distraught, not at all shocked, but distraught.

She shook her head, wanting to feel empathy for her best friend but at the same time, she wanted to shake her and yell that she had warned her of misfortunes with being Gino's conquest. Mia wanted to tell her that if she just listened to her she would be fine. Looking at her tear-stained face led her to do otherwise.

Mia forced a smile as she realized how excited Camryn was about being a mother.

"So he doesn't know that you're still pregnant?" Mia asked. Camryn shook her head no.

"I'm so scared Mia, I know he's going to try and kill me," Camryn admitted but Mia frowned.

"Don't say that, he must have loved you to some extent. He won't try and kill you."

"Oh, so now you think he must have loved me? You almost sound as naïve as I was," Camryn said with a smirk on her face, "He may have not raised the fist, but he had it raised," she said, referring to her run-in with Twan.

"Well, maybe he's calmed down since you've told him," Mia suggested trying to remain optimistic. Camryn let out a struggled laugh before shaking her head.

"Mia, I messed up, I really messed up," Camryn admitted. Mia rushed from the opposite side of the room and hugged her best friend. Camryn wrapped her arms around her and accepted.

"Camryn, this is how we learn," Mia spoke wisdom beyond her years. "God takes us through these things to make us better people. He isn't punishing you. He's developing you."

Camryn took in Mia's words with a nod. Mia waited until Camryn had stopped crying and wiped her face.

"You okay now, boo?" she asked. Camryn smiled before nodding. "Good," Mia said showcasing the smile that Camryn had missed so much over the last few months. Seeing Mia was like breathing clean air.

"Now, is Nana up because Momma wants to see her, I want you to meet Jayson, and Momma is cooking. With this load you are carrying, I'm sure you can eat," Mia said causing Camryn to laugh.

"Yeah, let me go see if she's dressed."

If you learn nothing else from your mistakes, know that there is a lesson to be learned. If you feel like you keep going through the same nonsense, it's just because you haven't learned your lesson yet. Stop trying to get through it....just learn through it.

Camryn smiled as Mia rambled on about university life. Camryn was proud of Mia, to say the least. After Mia ran out of news for Camryn, she started talking about her cousin, Jayson.

"Hopefully, you two will get along," Mia expressed, actually trying to convince herself of the same. Mia had confided her fear of Camryn's relationship with Gino to Jayson and Mia had to admit that the story wasn't too appealing. Jayson had assumed that Camryn was an ignorant little girl that Mia did not need to associate herself with, even though Mia tried numerous times to convince him otherwise. To Mia, Camryn was not an ignorant little girl, just a smart girl in love with the wrong guy. Although Mia loathed Camryn's attraction to Gino, she would never fault Camryn for being in love.

Mia wanted love, too.

"Why wouldn't we get along?" Camryn quizzed. "Huh?"

"You just said, hopefully we get along. Why wouldn't we?"

Mia shrugged her shoulders, not wanting to tell her best friend that her favorite cousin had already formed an opinion of her without knowing her. Camryn let the situation go and Mia inwardly sighed.

"So, do I get a niece or a nephew?" Mia asked laying her left hand on Camryn's stomach as her right controlled the car.

"I find out on my birthday," Camryn smiled.

"I hate that I have class," Mia pouted, "Maybe I'll skip and come home just for the day."

"No ma'am! You better not skip any class," Camryn commanded in all seriousness.

"Not even for your birthday?"

"No!"

"What about when the baby is born?" Mia asked with a smirk. Camryn wrinkled up her nose causing Mia to laugh.

"You should be on break then anyway," Camryn said. Mia frowned in defeat as she pulled up in front of her house. Even though she had an apartment at school, this was always home.

"Does Momma know?" Mia asked as she stopped at the front door and pointed down to Camryn's stomach.

Camryn nodded and Mia continued to unlock the large wooden door.

The familiar aroma of Miss Kathy's gumbo filled the air and both girls inhaled it. Mia smiled as the thought of sitting in front of a big bowl of gumbo entered her mind. Her mom always made the best gumbo because she added so much to it. Lobster, shrimp, oysters, smoked sausage, rice you name it and Miss Kathy had put it in a gumbo at one time or another.

Mia walked into the kitchen with Camryn in tow. Jayson was sitting at the kitchen table, typing away at his laptop. Miss Kathy had her back to the kitchen entrance as she checked on her progressing pot of gold. Mia turned towards Camryn and placed her left index finger over her mouth. Camryn nodded.

"Ma, is it done yet?" Mia asked causing both Jayson and her mom to turn around.

"Girl, you just left," Miss Kathy said, slightly annoyed before her eyes fell on who was behind her daughter. "Excuse me, do I know you?"

Everyone except Jayson, who didn't get the joke, laughed as Camryn walked from around Mia towards Miss Kathy. Miss Kathy fussed over her belly before actually giving her a hug.

"I see the weight is spreading nicely," Miss Kathy said, causing Camryn to smile.

"Thank God!"

"Camryn, this is my sister's baby, Jayson. Jayson, this is Mia's best friend Camryn," Miss Kathy introduced and Mia's heart fluttered a little as she stood back to watch the meeting. Jayson nonchalantly nodded, only glancing at Camryn for a split second and formed a smirk on his face. Camryn frowned.

"What's up," Jayson said after he was once again consumed with his own tasks. Camryn raised an eyebrow before responding.

"Hi," she said dryly. Mia sighed before grabbing a hold on Camryn's arm.

"Come on, I got you something," she announced. Camryn's features returned to a smile at the mention of gifts and followed her best friend out of the kitchen and into her old room.

Mia had been nostalgic since she had been home. As expected, her mom had not changed her room one bit; everything was exactly how Mia left it.

"Wow," Camryn commented, probably having the same exact reaction to the room that Mia had. Mia giggled as she went over to her things and pulled out a shoe box.

"I'm not sure if you can wear these now, I didn't know you were pregnant when I bought them," Mia solemnly announced, now feeling a little silly for buying the heels. Camryn quickly pulled the top off of the shoe box while sitting down on the edge of Mia's bed.

"These are fly," Camryn said with a smile.

"Do you really like them?"

Camryn gave Mia a look that she knew all too well. One thing Mia could say was that she always had great style. Camryn was always trying to steal Mia's clothes.

Mia laughed and smiled, glad that Camryn liked her gift.

Mia sat down next to Camryn and sighed.

"Boo, are you really okay?" Mia asked, concerned. Camryn sighed before a slow smile spread across her face and she nodded.

"I can't lie and say that I'm not scared for my child's and my life, but I'm content," Camryn confessed, "Actually excited."

Mia nodded at Camryn's maturity at the moment. She always saw her as naïve but her best friend was finally growing up. The two talked for a while before Miss Kathy loudly announced that the food was done.

"First we go to dinner, then we hit the movies. Now we back at my crib, off in the Jacuzzi. I'm kissing on your stomach, feeling on your booty. I want to have a party all over your body."

Twan, Gino, and Baywood strolled through the dark basement of Baby's house as if it they owned it. There were people everywhere but they all seemed to move out of their path. He wasn't particularly fond of the music that was being played, but he was only there for two reasons.

"There he is," Gino spoke into Twan's left ear just as he spotted Baby through his slightly narrowed eyelids. It took him a minute to respond to Gino as Twan found himself making his home in an eye ride up Baby's chocolate legs. He made brief eye contact with her before turning to Gino.

"Take Wood with you," Twan demanded. Gino frowned before he noticed Baby walking towards them. Gino nodded with a smile on his face before him and Baywood walked away towards their next transaction.

Twan leaned against the wall right under the basement stairs and watched Baby's journey towards him. She wore an irritated expression on her soft features as several people stopped her from getting there. Twan watched as her polite manner began to deteriorate with each guy that stopped her for a dance. It seemed as if every dude in the basement, whether he was with a chick or not, was hot on Baby's heels. Twan found himself actually wanting to jump to her defense and claim her as his, letting everyone for blocks around know that Baby was now untouchable. Twan knew better; he had to make sure that she was ready for his type of lifestyle. She was bad, but Twan wasn't stupid.

Twan took her irritated stature as an opportunity to check her appearance. He was very particular about how he felt a chick who was trying to get with him should dress. If he had to define it, his style of choice was Baby's to a tee. Twan slightly nodded in approval at her hooded black cut-off jacket that stopped right under her breasts and was unzipped to reveal a red and orange bra that matched the outline on the hood. The short black shorts she had on where red and orange around the waist. As usual, some red and orange Fusions graced her feet. Twan was even feeling the bun her hair was neatly done up in.

Baby finally got rid of her admirers and walked up on Twan, leaving little room between them.

"I've been waiting on you," Baby stated bluntly, not concerned about how she sounded. Twan glanced down at her breasts that were pressed up against his chest. "You see me?"

Twan nodded at her infamous line before telling her that she had it. A smile spread across Baby's face as she turned on the heels of her sneakers and grabbed the bottom of Twan's jacket from behind. Her model walk entranced Twan as she led him past all of the jealous guys and envious females. Baby stopped right in the middle of the basement floor as the DJ spun T.I. and Ciara's record, King and Queen. Twan knew that the nod Baby just gave the DJ meant that she was trying to get a point across.

Baby began to grind on Twan who, in return, tightly gripped her hips. She moved her hips in a suggestive way as she turned towards Twan and licked her lips.

Although Twan was enjoying the show, he wasn't one for dancing. He wanted to see where Baby's head was at before he decided to do anything. He was about to make big moves and if Baby played her hand right and did as he thought she would, she could be making moves with him.

"Take me to your room." Twan demanded. Baby nodded before walking off towards the stairs, Twan in tow.

Twan sat down on the edge of Baby's spacious bed and looked around. He watched as Baby closed and locked the door, the music from downstairs now muffled and low. She leaned against her bedroom door and glanced at Twan with a look of want.

"Why you on me, Tati?" Twan asked calling Baby by the name that was scribbled on her birth certificate. From the look on her face, Twan could tell that she was not in the least bit surprised that he had done his homework on her. Baby glanced at him for a second before her bottom lip slipped through her teeth.

"Should it matter, Antwan?"

Twan smiled because as simple as his nickname had been to his government, no one seemed to know it. Before Twan could respond, Baby was walking over towards him.

"The way I see it, we have a win-win situation here," Baby said as her bold persona allowed her to sit down on Twan's lap. "You need a bad chick and I need somebody strong, somebody that has clout on these streets."

"Why not go for Gino?" Twan tested her.

"He ain't the one I want," Baby said looking directly at Twan. "Gino is played out along with his lame girlfriend."

As she spoke, Baby began to kiss Twan's neck.

"You and me," she said leaning back to look at him, "We can make some moves."

Twan was sold before Baby even removed her jacket.

Jayson sat on the couch opposite of Mia and Camryn, highly annoyed. He watched the two giggle profusely and wondered what was so funny. Jayson had been sitting there for almost twenty minutes and he hadn't found anything funny.

Jayson had to admit that the stories he had heard about this girl that sat in front of him weren't as bad as he made them out to be. Mia always talked about what a good friend Camryn was to her, but her one problem stuck out to Jayson the most. She seemed naïve and ignorant to real life and those two were not good qualities to have in Jayson's eyes. Ignorance was the worst quality a girl could have.

"So what do you do Camden?" he asked causing the laughter from both girls to cease. Their attention turned to him as Mia huffed.

"Her name is Cam-RYN, Jayson," Mia corrected him. Camryn laid her hand on Mia's knee to let her know it wasn't that serious.

"I work at Wireless Communications, we are authorized dealers for AT&T and Sprint," Camryn answered.

"You don't go to school?" Jayson asked. It was Camryn's turn to frown.

"Actually I take online classes right now."

"When did you have them switched?" Mia asked turning to her best friend. Jayson glanced at Mia as Camryn's attention went back to her.

"When I got out of the hospital," Camryn answered, "Nana thought it would be safer."

"Are you hiding from someone?" Jayson asked.

"Jayson!" Mia yelled.

"Is there a reason you are all in my business?" Camryn asked as her annoyed attitude began to show.

"I'm just trying to figure out why my cousin calls you her best friend."

"What have you been telling him?" Camryn quizzed Mia who in turn glared at Jayson.

"You are so out of line!"

"Mia, what have you been telling him?" Camryn asked once again.

"Cam, it's not like that, I swear!" Mia pleaded as Jayson watched on, slightly amused. "I just vented to him when I hadn't talked to you in a while. I was scared that Gino had done something to you."

Camryn sighed as Mia sat up, slightly turned towards her in an apologizing position. Camryn shook her head before smiling.

"I'm not mad at you, but your cousin is out of line so I think it's about time for me to go."

"Nice meeting you," Jayson spat out. Camryn just ignored him but Mia jumped up.

"Cam..."

"It's cool Mia, I need to go to the drug store and get my pills anyway." Camryn said, waving Jayson's behavior off.

"Let me take you," Mia said grabbing her purse and not waiting for an answer. She frowned at Jayson before her and Camryn left out the front door.

Jayson got comfortable across the couch as he thought about nothing in particular. He wondered what made girls go for guys who would physically abuse them in the first place. Some of them even seemed to be prone to getting beat.

It was always the girl that had nothing and wanted it all. Any baller could attract her with his cars, clothes, or status and have her head over heels in love. Jayson shook his head at the thought.

He was a well-educated man, treated all women with respect and half the time he was overlooked. He knew not to be bitter about the situation though. All of the girls he had come in contact with so far were not what he thought of as wife material. Jayson was 25 and was not into playing games. He was a semester away from his Master's degree in Public Relations and he was ready to start a family. Jayson just wasn't sure if it was the women he met that were hindering him, or himself.

We judge others by our own faults. We see their downfalls and prey on their weaknesses to make ourselves feel redeemed for our own. This only covers our problems temporarily. We will have to face them soon.

Gino sat impatiently on his couch in his empty home. Tameka had been gone all morning and instead of him calling her, he decided to get some much handled business out of the way. Gino made a few calls to have an emergency meeting and everyone seemed to be running late. Gino hated people being late for meetings.

His dark eyes looked up towards the large flat screen television that hung firmly on the white wall across from where he sat. A newscaster was telling the predictions of an upcoming storm and the areas that would be hit. There were heavy thunderstorm watches taking place in the county and surrounding ones. Gino frowned at the thought of the day being worse than it already was. He sighed while sitting back, throwing his left hand over his eyes. The headache that had been forming since he woke up was gaining strength.

Gino had been thinking of his lost lover for the past few days. He missed her in a way. She was always the one who did as she was told. Camryn always had a hot meal ready for him when he came at any time of the day, never resisted him sexually. Gino could not understand what would possess her to defy him in the way she had.

It was her fault that it had ended that way.

On several occasions Gino had thought of contacting Camryn. He figured she would be in the right mindset now, even okay that she was no longer carrying his child. He knew he would probably have to explain Tameka's actions, seeing as she had taken it upon herself to approach Camryn. Gino also wanted to set Tameka back in her place but since she hadn't approached him with the Camryn situation, he figured he would leave it alone for now.

Gino cursed himself for thinking about her. Although Tameka had been playing the perfect wife for the last couple of weeks, there was something different in Gino's relationship with Camryn. Something he didn't want to admit that he needed. He struggled with himself because of part of him felt like Camryn should have been trying to reach out to him. After all, she was the one who messed everything up by getting pregnant.

A mellow doorbell sang out as Gino's company was announced, drawing him out of his struggling mindset. Knowing that Tameka was absent from their home, Gino reluctantly got up from his seat and went to answer the door. He pulled it up and walked away, not even greeting the two that stood on the other side.

"You're a lousy host," Baywood joked as he and Twan joined Gino in the basement, where all business was conducted. Twan let out a deep belly chuckle as Gino glared at Baywood.

"We need to cut this snake's head off." Gino announced.

"Yeah, that's not simple if you don't know whose head is the snake's head," Baywood retorted. Gino sighed in frustration at the truth in Baywood's statement. The snake Gino had been hunting down for several months was smart. All of the tests he had put his camp through weren't working. He needed to think of something quick before the snake bit harder.

Gino glanced at Twan and wondered where his mind was. He hadn't seen him in the last few days and Gino was accustomed to Twan being around.

"Where you been?" Gino asked as his and Baywood's eyes averted to Twan. He looked up at both of them to see who the question was directed to and smiled.

"Taking care of some business," Twan replied, stretching out the last word in his sentence.

"What type of business, I haven't seen you since that party…" Gino stopped and answered his own question. A sinister smile spread across his face as he realized what business his boy had been taking care of.

"You serious? You pulled her?" Baywood questioned, causing Gino to frown.

"Of course he pulled her, you see how tough she was on him."

Twan chuckled as the talk of Baby filled the room. Her name was often accompanied by a lot of talk.

Before the three could discuss anything else, a long bang sounded from upstairs as a few things against the wall crashed.

"Where the hell you at!"

The three looked at each other as Tameka's voice echoed through the house. Gino growled as he jogged up the basement steps, Baywood and Twan in toe. All three of them stopped to see a broke down Tameka in tears, glass lay around her feet from the front door that was shattered.

Gino's eyes turned red to match Tameka's at the sight of his door.

"Have you lost your damn mind?"

Tameka ignored the question as she flung several pictures in his direction, they whirled to his feet but his eyes stayed on her. Twan looked down at one picture that had landed in front of him and his eyes widened.

"Oh shit!"

"That bitch is still pregnant!" Tameka screamed as the hurt she was feeling came out in her voice. Gino froze as soon as the words left her mouth. Baywood looked around lost.

"What did you say?" Gino asked as Twan handed him the picture. Gino's heart skipped a beat as Camryn's full face came into view. It was a picture of her at the grocery store, one hand picking up a box on the top shelf and the other lay under her stomach, supporting the bump that was visible at the rise of her shirt.

"Yeah, your bitch is still pregnant!"

Gino quickly gave Twan a questioningly look, who was still confused himself.

"You told me…"

"I did!" Twan yelled defending himself. There was no way a baby could live through the blows he gave Camryn that night. "There's no way."

"Guess again!" Tameka yelled as her leg began to shake.

The newscast was right, there was a heavy thunderstorm on its way.

Camryn sighed as her son sat on top of her bladder in a tight ball. He had been very active and Camryn was the complete opposite.

Camryn was looking over her transcript but had stopped to take a break. She tapped the small picture that proclaimed proof of her son and smiled.

Camryn's 20th birthday had come and gone. As suspected, the only highlight was finding out that she would indeed be birthing a son. She wasn't shocked in the least bit. Camryn was strong enough in her faith to know that the message she received from her mother was from God.

Camryn frowned as a small lump became visible through the red tank top she was wearing.

"Why are you bothering me, son?" she joked before moving on her side.

Camryn had been trying to figure out if she had enough credits to get her associates degree in Communications at the end of the semester. Nana and she had been discussing a move. Camryn had to admit that her reason for not wanting to leave was her naïve dream that Gino would come to his senses, but she had finally given that up.

King ran in and rubbed against Camryn's leg. She leaned over and scooped him up, placing him on her lap. He lay there, next to her unborn son.

Camryn found herself bored while waiting for Nana to return. She played with King until the doorbell rang.

Camryn waddled through the living room, breathing heavily by the time she reached the door.

Swinging it open, Camryn's heart almost jumped out of her chest to see her ex-lover standing as fine as he could be on a particular day.

Gino leaned coolly against the door frame, his chiseled jaw straight and tight. His dark sunglasses hid the cold stare Camryn knew he was giving her.

Camryn wasn't sure what to do as he removed his glasses and stared at her pregnant belly. There was no way to hide their love child from him. Camryn was terrified.

They stood staring at each other, both not knowing how to take their reunion. Gino stood up straight.

"You're still pregnant," he said stepping forwards, inviting himself into the atmosphere that had erased everything about him, except for his child.

"Gino I don't want anything from you," Camryn panicked, "I won't even say he's yours."

"How are you still pregnant?" he asked while closing Camryn's front door. She backed up into the living room as he walked further in.

"You can't kill him," Camryn said wrapping both of her arms around her stomach. "I can't kill him, no one can."

Camryn watched Gino stare at her in confusion. She looked away as nostalgic feelings tried to force their way out of the box her heart was holding them in.

"You're messing things up for me, Camryn."

"Why are you so selfish?"

As soon as those words were yelled from Camryn's mouth, Gino had her pinned to the nearest wall by her neck. Camryn struggled against his strength but looked him right in the eyes.

"You can try all you want, but this baby is going to be born regardless of who doesn't want him to be," Camryn said. Gino's vice grip on her small neck tightened.

"Surviving Twan made you tough, huh?" Gino joked. Camryn's nose flared.

"You know what Gino, go to hell. I can't believe how stupid I was. I can't believe I let you trick me into loving you."

"Camryn, this wasn't love," Gino said letting Camryn's neck go and turning his head. Camryn pulled his arm to make him face her.

"Oh really, paying most of these bills, laying up with me every night, watching me sleep in the morning, bringing me lunch and flowers at work, rubbing my feet, calling me all the time while you were out of town. That's not love?"

Gino smacked his lips as he began to walk towards the front door. Camryn quickly maneuvered around him and pressed her back to it, blocking his escape.

"Or is it because I wasn't laid up in the house like Tameka is? Is that why this wasn't love?" Camryn screamed as tears streamed down her face. She didn't want him to see her cry but it was too late.

"Get out of the way," Gino whispered.

"Why, so you can send Twan back to finish what you started, what we started?"

Gino stepped back and watched Camryn with wide eyes. She had never been this way with him and Camryn knew he was shocked. She had waited nearly five months to get this off her chest. No matter how much she told herself she wasn't stressing Gino's actions, the reality was the total opposite.

Camryn roughly wiped her face before sighing.

"Was that all I meant to you, Gino, just a kick to the stomach?"

"Camryn you weren't being rational," Gino said defending his decisions.

"I'm pregnant with your baby!" she yelled.

"Tameka flipped when she found out."

Camryn's heart stopped for a second time as her mind recalled the day at the mall where her ignorance was revealed in the form of a happy couple shopping together. She rolled her eyes and threw her arms up in the air in a mock surrender.

"I'm not even going to be naïve about this anymore than I already have. I know now that I was just your dip and you had no intentions of cuffing me. I get it Gino, but why are you here, huh?"

Camryn watched as Gino's eyelids lowered and widened again. He ran his hand down his chocolate face and licked his lips. He looked from the couch back to Camryn and she nodded quickly. Gino walked over and sat down but Camryn stood her ground in front of the front door.

"Tameka has been tailing you."

"I know. She came here last month." Camryn said crossing her arms below her chest and above her son. Gino shook his head.

"She has pictures of you at the grocery store and work. That's how she found out you were still pregnant."

Camryn was slightly amused by how much of Tameka's time she had consumed.

"That doesn't explain why you are here."

No matter how much Gino said that his relationship with Camryn wasn't serious, Camryn knew otherwise. Gino missed her and as much as he didn't want to show that, it was painfully obvious to Camryn. It helped to know she had been missed.

"Tameka's on a rampage, her and her girls have been planning some shit and I been trying to see what's going on but she hasn't talked to me since she found out."

"That's just like a female to blame the chick," Camryn thought.

"You should leave town."

Camryn laughed at Gino's warning, reminding him of what she had said earlier about no one being able to kill her son. It didn't matter that her and Nana were thinking of relocating. She wasn't going to let anyone run her away.

She unlocked the front door but did not open it.

"You can leave now, we don't need you trying to be nice to us," Camryn said. Gino rolled his eyes.

"You are being real stupid, but I guess I can't expect much else from you," Gino said before getting up and quickly walking over to where Camryn stood. He got close to Camryn, pressing slightly against her belly. "It's a shame you don't know the difference between love and fucking."

Camryn wanted to cry but she saw no use.

"I could say the same for you," she said as she pushed Gino off of her and opened the front door. As soon as he walked out of it, Camryn closed and locked it.

Finally alone, Camryn's eyes immediately spilled over with tears as her hand lay above her heart and the other supporting her belly. She slowly walked over to the couch and sat down while taking deep breaths to get her heart beat back to normal. Camryn wasn't sure if Gino had been there to harm her or make up with her and the end result was more horrific than she expected. He was a monster to Camryn, but why had he warned her of Tameka's plans. Was he part of the plan? Camryn sat back against the couch and began to pray for understanding. This was definitely more than she could handle.

When a relationship ends on bad terms, separation over time always heals the wounds. Out of sight, out of mind always reigns true. When that separation is broken, things take a turn for the worse. Feelings, intuitions, emotions, and logic begin to intertwine themselves with each other, blurring the lines of reality and hopes. This sets you up for the unbearable.

Tribute to a Woman

The sun beamed through the thick stained glass of the church as the harmonies of the youth choir sang about peace. Miss Marie gripped Camryn's hand as she swayed side to side, closing her eyes every few seconds.

"Peace, I give to you my peace. I leave with you, when trouble, trouble comes in your life. Peace I leave with you."

Camryn sniffed as her eyes began to water. It had been several days since Gino's visit and she was paranoid. Everywhere she went, Camryn felt that Tameka would be popping up to hurt her. She hated feeling like this. Although she told Gino she wasn't going anywhere, the idea of leaving town was starting to sound really good.

Camryn tried to smile as Nana patted her hand in a gesture of comfort.

Before church, Nana had made the suggestion that Camryn go to school with Mia next semester. Nana's sister had invited them to come live with her and in a few months, Nana would be relocating.

The plan was that Camryn would stay with them until the baby was old enough to go to daycare.

Camryn wasn't sure what to do. She wanted to get out of town but not living with Nana would be something she wasn't used to.

Camryn decided to not think about anything. She wanted to enjoy the service because she had been dreading leaving the house every day. She had no control over what Tameka would do and she knew worrying herself about it was not going to help.

As the choir continued to sing, Camryn thought back to the vision of her mother as she did often. She believed that her son did have a calling on his life, but at the same time she wondered about her own. Her child could not be harmed, but what about her? One trip to the hospital was enough for Camryn. It was hard to be strong in this situation.

"Sister Camryn, can you come up here please?"

Camryn's head shot up as she looked towards the voice that was calling her attention. She looked around as if he did not just call her name. He lowered his head, keeping his eye on her and motioned her once again with his index finger.

Nana released Camryn's hand and gently pushed on her thigh. Camryn sighed as she pulled on the pew in front of her with both hands. Camryn straightened her dress out as she stepped past Nana and out into the aisle. She slowly made her way towards the Pastor as a few of the ushers and the first lady of the church stood near.

Camryn had seen this scene play out many times.

Once she got there, Pastor Randall grabbed both of her hands and gave her a reassuring smile.

"You don't need to be scared," he said. Camryn began to tear up as she felt the first lady place her hand on the small of her back.

"Do you hear me?" he asked. Camryn nodded. "God has not given you the spirit of fear. He knows what he wants from you and he will protect you. Baby, put your hand on her stomach," he instructed his wife.

Camryn smiled as First Lady Randall gently rubbed her belly. Pastor Randall turned his wireless microphone off.

"You don't need me to repeat what God has already revealed to you, but He realizes that you need support. You need to stay in Him, Camryn. Stay in Him," he repeated. Camry nodded. "Raise your hands."

As Camryn raised both arms and the pastor placed one hand on Camryn's forehead and the other on top of his wife's that lay on her stomach, Camryn felt a weight lift off her shoulder.

She cried as prayers went up for her. She cried out for strength. She cried out for some type of guidance and she cried for understanding. After crying so much, Camryn cried in gratefulness. She knew that God had her situation under control. She even felt bad for doubting him.

We get messages from God all the time. We believe them but never totally leave the situation up to Him. Sometimes, we just need a little reassurance.

The slightly darkened skin on Camryn's belly moved as a lumpy wave came through. She looked down at her hand that was rubbing her belly in soothing, circular motion. Her mouth fell slightly open as the movements continued.

"This little boy is going crazy," Camryn spoke into the phone that was glued to her ear. Mia giggled.

"What is he doing?"

"Kicking and flipping, all types of stuff," Camryn said smiling.

"He does all of that?"

"Yes, Nana says that's how Momma was when she was pregnant with her."

"How was church?" Mia asked as Camryn flipped through channels.

"It was good, great actually. You?"

"Jayson's church is nice, but I miss home."

"Yeah, first lady asked about you today," Camryn told her.

"I'll probably be coming to visit again soon," Mia said, "So you're coming next weekend right?"

"Yes ma'am, my vacation hours were approved."

"I don't see how you are still working,"

"Mia, I'm not even seven months yet," Camryn said laughing. Mia groaned.

"I would be about three, trying to go on maternity leave."

Camryn gripped her side as she laughed harder. Mia went on about how lazy she was going to be whenever she got pregnant. Camryn shook her head knowing that Mia was probably right. The phone beeped and Camryn pulled it away from her ear to see it was a call from the church.

"Mia, Nana is calling. I'll call you back a little later."

"Okay."

"Hey Nana, what's up?"

"You may want to come get a plate, there are a lot of people coming in."

"Oh, make it for me and I'll be down there in a minute!"

Nana laughed as they said goodbye.

Camryn slipped on some dark green sweatpants over her shorts and her white sneakers. She grabbed her purse and headed out of the door.

Baby unwrapped her long legs from around Twan's waist causing him to drop his arm that was holding it up. Twan sighed, trying to pick it back up but Baby shook her head no.

"I wasn't done," Twan repeated against the skin on her neck. Baby licked her lips but pushed him to the side.

"Yes you are, sir. We have business to take care of."

Twan slid his hands behind his head and smiled. Baby stretched her arms out as she pulled herself to sit up against the marble headboard. Twan licked his lips as the white cotton sheet fell from her chocolate skin and revealed his newest candy. Baby rolled her eyes as she pulled the sheet tighter around her frame.

She slid open the top drawer of her nightstand and pulled out an opened pack of Newports. Twan frowned as she slid one of the cigarettes between her thick lips and held a match up to it.

Baby closed her eyes as she sucked in her cancer before blowing smoke from her mouth.

"So finish telling me what happened," she said, crossing her legs under the sheet. Twan laughed a little while remembering what happened.

"Tameka starts crying about how she was supposed to be the one to have Gino's seed or whatever," Twan started and Baby nodded. "Gino's pissed trying to calm Tameka down without whooping her ass while I'm trying to figure out how and the hell this baby lived."

Baby looked at Twan and wrinkled her nose.

"You said you kicked her?"

"Man, I did everything but kill that girl," Twan said, "Anyway, Tameka's flipping out on the phone and next thing we know her girls are over there. Gino blows up and cusses Tameka out, telling her she better have his door fixed by the time he gets back and we bounced."

"Where you go?" Baby asked.

"To the trap," Twan said as his eyelids began to hide his tired eyes. Baby smashed her cigarette in the crystal ashtray before straddling his waist.

"Get up, no time to sleep," she said gripping his muscled arms. Twan smirked but did not open his eyes.

"I'm chilling today, while Gino takes care of the crib."

"And waste a whole day? You need to let him know that you can handle a day without him, you know how everything runs. The whole camp shouldn't have to miss out on today's money because Gino can't control his chick," Baby said as she leaned down and massaged Twan's temples with the tips of her fingers. Twan gripped the smooth meat right above her hips, finally opening his eyes.

He thought about what she said and realized she was right. He knew that Gino hated losing money but he hated not being around either. They were boys though, all the way back to pushing weight for a local dealer to get sneakers. Twan nodded subconsciously to Baby's idea. She smiled.

"Good, now if you promise to get up, Momma will give you something to get you through your day," she said letting the sheet fall from its place. Twan ran his hands up her stomach and cupped each breast in his hand. Baby bit her lip as he sat up and kissed her neck.

"That's all you had to say to get me up," Twan said as Baby giggled.

Tameka stared enviously at the scene that played out before her. She and Tani, her older cousin, were sitting on the couch waiting for Lori to finish sucking face with her man. Tameka was happy for Lori that Chase was out of jail, but when he and Gino came in the house interrupting their plans, Tameka felt that Lori could have saved the public display of affection.

Tameka had known Chase ever since she had known Gino. She actually noticed him first. He was tall and built like a football player, not too big but he was cut. He had black dreads that never went past his shoulder then, since coming home he had a clean fade. His caramel skin was a few shades lighter than Gino's and black eyes. Jacob looked a lot like him.

When Tameka met them she saw Chase first, but as soon as Gino came into the room she knew she wanted him. After they hit it off, Tameka introduced Chase to Lori.

Tameka huffed as Chase pulled Lori's thick frame into him and she let out a girlish giggle.

"Fuck much?" Tani whispered. Tameka shook her head.

"These hips are screaming for another baby," Chase said as he bit Lori's neck.

"Not if they daddy keeps going to jail," she whined. Chase slid his left hand around her neck and guided her lips to his. Lori stood on her toes and kissed him harder. Tameka rolled her eyes.

Tameka's eyes fell to the kitchen where Gino appeared in the door frame with an annoyed look on his face.

"Chase," he called. Chase let go of Lori's lips and smirked. "Come on."

Lori pouted as Chase turned her around and tapped her butt and she walked back over to the couch.

"A dude can't greet his old lady without you hating?" Chase called to Gino, who had already walked back into the kitchen. Lori sat down with a sigh. She turned to see Tameka and Tani staring at her.

"Dang, excuse me," Lori said sitting back. Tani laughed but Tameka just shook her head. "It wasn't like you figured anything out anyway."

"How are you going to do anything without G finding out you did it?" Tani whispered while looking towards the kitchen.

"I almost don't care."

"Well, I think you better," Lori said, "We all know you aren't going to leave him. If you do anything to that girl he is going to know and I'm sure the shit will hit the fan even harder."

"Lori shut up," Tani said but Tameka knew that Lori was right.

"Let me think about it," Tameka said. Tani frowned.

"What is there to think about? This sideline chick is having G's first born. Everybody around here knows about you, Meka. I don't care where you from. That is mad disrespectful."

Lori shook her head as she watched Tameka feed into what Tani was saying. She hated how dumb her best friend had gotten over a dude. Lori felt like she was losing Tameka mentally. Lori didn't know what to do but she knew she had to think of something. As long as Tani was feeding Tameka this mess, Lori knew that this would turn out bad.

Camryn inhaled as the cool breeze filled her car. She had been riding around for about an hour with nowhere in particular to go. Camryn had been in the house for so long that she forgot how nice the breeze was at night.

Camryn glanced down at her stomach that was almost touching the steering wheel and smiled. She had two and a half more months of her term and she would finally get to see her son.

Camryn had to admit that she was very nervous about labor and motherhood in general. Nana had always taken care of her. Sure, she helped with bills and little things but never had she been independent of Nana until her most recent hospital visits. Another life would be depending on her to do the right things and that scared her.

Camryn made a turn towards the high school she used to go to and shook her head. She rode past the parking lot that Gino would floss in daily, catching the attention of several girls and the jealousy of most guys. She rode past the park next to the football field where Gino had first approached her and she turned him down. At that same park, just a few weeks later, would be the same spot that Camryn accepted Gino's offer to take her out.

She remembered how charming and smooth Gino was with her. How she was always impressed by the way he carried himself. Camryn knew now that his persona was based on the fact that he thought too much of himself. Everyone was below Gino, in his eyes and she wished she would have seen that sooner.

Camryn took her wish back as soon as it filled her thoughts. She knew that there was great reason to why she was impregnated with Gino's child. Camryn knew that her son would have all of the wonderful qualities that made Gino her first love and she would fight to death to make sure the bad qualities were not even an option.

Camryn pulled into the parking lot and turned the car off. She locked the doors and turned her radio up slightly. Reclining her seat back a little, she closed her eyes and wrapped her arms around her belly. She didn't get much peace anywhere else. Even at home she felt a little unsure. Camryn just wanted peace. She even wanted peace for Gino. She knew the difference between the real him and the Gino who had deemed himself street king. They had two very different personalities and Camryn knew that each one was fighting for the top spot.

Camryn pulled out her cell phone and dialed Gino's number but did not hit send. She wasn't surprised that she had remembered it even though it had been several months since she erased it from her contact list. Camryn held down the end button until the number disappeared and turned her phone off instead.

"Twenty years old and fighting for my life," Camryn whispered to herself in the mirror before she slid her seat back up into a comfortable driving position and turned the car back on. As Camryn made her way back around to the front of the high school she turned the radio back down. She usually did when other cars were around and two had been on the same street as her.

Camryn squinted her eyes as the car behind her got closer and their lights grew brighter. She frowned and wondered if the driver was drunk and turned a few corners to get away from them. When she looked up the car was still behind her.

Camryn panicked as she realized what was going on. The car didn't have any license plates and no matter what street she turned on, the car behind her turned as well. A tear slid down Camryn's eye as she secured her seat belt and tried to figure out the quickest way to the police station because going home would do no good.

The car behind her bumped into her and her son kicked inside of her as her heart rate sped up. She laid her right hand on her stomach as her left one gripped the wheel.

"It's okay baby," she whispered as the car bumped into her again, this time a little harder. Camryn's little car shook as she tried to speed up. The car slid into the left lane and sped up as well. They got on the side of Camryn and she tried to see who it was but the windows were pitch black. Camryn began to pray as the car rammed into her driver's side and pushed her off into a ditch.

Her air bag pushed its way out of its compartment and stung her face. She closed her eyes and moaned as she felt the blood flow down her forehead and everything went silent. She couldn't see and she couldn't move but she could hear doors slamming. She tried to yell as she heard footsteps in the grass but nothing came out. All she could do was cry.

Her car door shook a little and Camryn realized someone was trying to open it.

"Can you see her? Is she dead?" Camryn heard a voice say.

"We didn't hit her that hard stupid," another voice said.

"The damn door is stuck!" Camryn cried harder as she matched the last voice to Tameka's.

"Hurry up before somebody comes!"

"Go around to the other side and see if it's open,"

"I'm going to shoot this door off in a second,"

"Tameka, G's here!"

Camryn tried to move at the mention of Gino's name as the three girls got silent. She could hear Gino's truck pulling up and several doors opening and slamming.

She could hear a lot of commotion as if they were all running around her car.

"I should kill your stupid ass, what did you do?" Gino's voice spat. Camryn cried harder as she realized that

Gino had come to stop whatever Tameka was trying to do to her. He had tried to warn her and now he was saving her.

"Don't come at me like that, this is your mess!" Tameka said.

Her words were cut off before Camryn heard a thud against Gino's truck.

"Gino, let her go, she can't breathe!" one of the voices from earlier said.

Camryn felt a pain in her leg and her arm that were pinned up against the door. She wanted to yell, besides the fact that she couldn't, she was scared to.

"G, you don't have time for this man," Camryn heard Twan's voice yell.

"Twan, take them to the house and make sure they don't leave," Gino said, "Baywood help me get her out."

Camryn stopped trying to move as her car shook harder than before. She struggled to move but everything became blurry. The last thing she remembered was Gino's hand on her arm.

Gino looked down at an unconscious Camryn and shook his head. She had cuts on her forehead as well as up and down her arms and left leg. Gino lifted up her shirt and examined her belly. He slightly smiled at the roundness of it.

"Which hospital?" Baywood asked from the driver's seat as he sped down the highway.

"Mercy," Gino said, his eyes still stuck on Camryn's belly. He swallowed the saliva that had formed in his mouth as he hand gently slid across the very center of her stomach. He pulled his hand back when he felt a small kick. He eyes were fixated on the spot as the baby kicked again. Gino had never seen anything like it and wasn't sure how to react. After a few minutes, Gino put his hand back on the same spot but this time he didn't feel a thing. Gino slowly pulled Camryn's shirt back down before looking up towards her face. His eyes widened as he saw Camryn staring at him. She didn't blink once or move; she just stared at him. Gino looked around the back seat and tried to avoid her eyes but she did not lose her gaze.

"We're here," Baywood said pulling up at the emergency entrance. He parked the car and ran towards the door yelling for someone to come help him. Gino pushed the backdoor open and got out with Camryn in his arms. Her eyes had closed again and he wasn't sure if she was conscious or not.

"Sir what happened?" a nurse asked as a few people came out with a stretcher.

"I found her in her car in a ditch," Gino said as he gently laid Camryn down on the stretcher. The people holding it immediately began to check her pulse and eyes. Baywood jumped back into the car as Gino just stood there.

"Come on man," Baywood said honking the horn. Gino shook his head and hopped in the passenger seat. Baywood sped off.

Gino knew that Tameka was crazy. He knew that she was planning to hurt Camryn some way but he could never figure it out. All morning she had been acting weird and Gino figured it had something to do with Camryn. She left the house in such a hurry that Gino ended up following her to make sure that she didn't do anything stupid. She had gotten away from them for a few blocks and when he caught up with her, he found her trying to drag Camryn out of her car with Tani and one of her hood rat friends. Gino knew that if he hadn't showed up that they would have done damage to Camryn once they got her out that car.

"Take me to the house," Gino said running his hand down his face before he balled his fist up.

Tameka paced the carpeted floor as Twan watched her from his seat on the couch. Gino told him to drop Tani and her goon off so that when he got there it would just be him and Tameka. Twan called Chase to let him know that business had been postponed for a few hours. Twan knew that Gino was going to go crazy when he got to the house and he had to admit that he was anxious to see it.

Twan laughed as tears ran down Tameka's face.

"You think this is funny don't you?" Tameka asked.

"I think you're funny," Twan said pointing at her.

"Don't push me today," Tameka said. Twan laughed aloud.

"Tameka you're full of shit, you don't scare me even a little bit," Twan said. Tameka stopped in front of him and crossed her arms.

"You haven't seen me pissed, don't push me," Tameka said.

Twan felt a little sorry for her. He tilted his head before pulling a blunt from his ear.

"If you haven't figured it out by now, everybody knows you aren't shit," Twan said. "Everybody around here knows that Tameka is Gino's bitch, she only does what Gino tells her."

Tameka said nothing at Twan dissected her life.

"The fact that you went after the chick only shows that you are jealous of her. She has something you don't have, hell she has a lot you don't have, including the one you're fighting for."

"Gino loves me," Tameka said.

"Love ain't shit, Tameka. Grow up."

"Go to hell!"

"Tameka, do you honestly think you're still here because he loves you? Gino doesn't give a damn about anybody, especially not a female."

"Well, since you're so damn smart, why am I still here?" Tameka said and Twan smiled.

"You're still here because you won't leave."

Before Tameka could respond, someone banged on the front door. Tameka got up and answered it. Lori ran in the house with Chase on her hills.

"What did you do? Tell me you didn't hurt that girl?"

"Why are you worried about her?" Tameka asked.

"Meka, don't be dumb! He's going to hurt you for whatever you did to her, now what did you do?" Lori asked. The front door slammed and everyone looked to see Gino standing in front of it. Chase pulled Lori's arm so that she wasn't standing next to Tameka anymore. Tameka frowned as she saw the look in his eye.

"You love her don't you?"

Gino walked over to Tameka, wrapped his hand around her throat, and pinned her to the wall. Tameka's eyes widened as she tried to move his hand.

"Whatever is wrong with your mind, I suggest you get it right," Gino said as he pushed his index finger into her forehead. Tameka's head banged against the wall and she closed her eyes.

"Why are you doing this to me? After everything I've done for you, all the shit I put up with?" Tameka yelled as she fought against him to get off the wall.

"Oh, you must have it real bad sitting up in this big house with two cars to drive, hundreds of designer clothes, jewelry out the ass. Damn how horrible it is to be Tameka!" Gino yelled in her face.

"I'm not Tameka anymore!"

"You're damn right," Gino said.

"Fuck you!"

As soon as those words left Tameka's mouth, the fight began. She took the first swing at Gino and landed on his jaw. Once he realized what she had done, he returned the same punch. Tameka's back hit the wall as Gino backhanded her to the ground. Lori struggled in Chase's arms as she yelled for Gino to stop. Twan just watched.

Tameka struggled to her feet but Gino wrapped his hand around her ponytail and swung her into the wall. Tameka twisted her body and kneed Gino in his balls. Gino released her ponytail and Tameka charged at him, both of them falling to the floor. She struggled to pull her knife from her pocket but as soon as Gino saw it, he knocked it out of her hand.

Gino flipped them over, pinned Tameka to the ground and wrapped both of his arms tightly around her throat.

"Just admit it," Tameka choked out.

"It's not about her, it's about you disrespecting me," Gino said. "I told you to leave shit alone, I'm taking care of you, not her."

"It's always about you," Tameka whispered as she started losing air. Twan smirked as Lori broke from Chase's grip. Everyone thought she would try to fight Gino but instead, she got down on her knees by Tameka and looked up at Gino.

"G, I've never asked you for nothing, we don't get along, I damn near hate you but please don't do this," Lori said placing her hands on top of Gino's. Tameka's eyes pleaded with Gino as he looked at Lori. Tears fell down her eyes as Tameka began to cough.

"G, she loves you so much. You have to understand how she feels. She loves you more than she loves herself and she wanted to have your baby. She wanted to give you that when you were ready. To see some girl walking around carrying your seed is killing her."

"I don't want any kids," Gino said as he grip slightly loosened. The blood from Tameka's lip covered his hands.

"It doesn't matter G, you have one on the way and it's not by the one who would do anything for you. Tameka would do anything for you, even try to fix what you couldn't."

Gino looked from Lori to Tameka as Lori slid her hands under Gino's and tried to lift them. After a few seconds, he let her. Tameka rolled over on her side as she coughed, gently rubbing her throat as Lori wiped the blood off of her face.

Gino looked down at Tameka as he caught his breath.

"Ay, we need to leave," Twan said and Chase nodded. Gino straightened off his shirt before following Chase and Twan out the front door.

Tameka broke out in tears as Lori tried to soothe her.

"I knew I shouldn't have let you listen to Tani's ass," Lori mumbled as she pulled Tameka into her lap. "It's going to be okay, Meka," Lori said trying not to cry.

"It's not," Tameka said shaking her head. "It's not going to be okay, Lori."

Lori didn't respond because she knew that Tameka was right. It wasn't going to be okay.

What happens when you think what you've decided to do is the right thing? It either turns out to be the right thing and the situation isn't as worse or it turns out that you were horribly wrong. You complicate the situation as far as it can go and now you can't take it back. Words that were exchanged, fists that were thrown, feelings that were admitted cannot be taken back. Your position is compromised and you have no idea what is going to happen. The little pride you had left, is gone.

Camryn lay still with her eyes closed as she listened to the slow beeping of her heart monitor. She pushed her head against the hard, thin pillow as her right hand gripped the side of her stomach.

Her left arm was itching and Camryn felt the IV in her arm move slightly. Once again, she found herself laid out in a hospital bed because of her feelings for Gino.

This time, Camryn's feelings weren't hurt because Gino had betrayed her. She wasn't scared about Tameka finding out about the baby and trying something crazy. Camryn wasn't shocked that the whole ordeal happened.

Camryn was confused.

The only thing that Camryn could think of was being in the backseat of Gino's truck with him on the way to the hospital. Camryn couldn't wrap her mind around how she felt about Gino rubbing her belly. She had been awake since they got her in the truck. Now, she was sure that Gino had a heart. She just wasn't sure what that meant at the time.

When a nurse came in, Camryn opened her eyes to reveal that she was conscious. After the nurse advised Camryn that despite a few cuts and bruises she was fine, she was free to go.

Camryn took her time calling a cab to get home. She hadn't even thought about what she was going to do about her car. It hadn't crossed her mind until she realized she had no way home. The cab ride was shorter than expected and as Camryn looked up at her home, she prayed that Nana wasn't awake.

It was going on five in the morning and Camryn knew Nana usually woke up between now and seven.

She crept into the house but relaxed once she realized that Nana was still sleeping. Camryn decided to pass on taking a shower until later and went to sleep.

She jumped as her cell phone rang against her thigh. She groaned as she looked at the front screen and saw an unfamiliar number calling her at nine in the morning.

"Hello?"

"Cam..."

Camryn's eyes shot open as Gino's voice filled her left ear. She didn't respond.

"Come outside."

Camryn shut her phone before getting out of her bed and walking over to her window. Her hand flew to her mouth as her eyes followed the length of Gino's truck and her own car sitting in front of it. Camryn slid on her shoes and went outside.

Ignoring Gino's presence as he leaned against the hood of his truck, Camryn supported her back and belly with each hand as she walked around her car in awe. There wasn't a scratch or dent anywhere.

If it hadn't been so vivid in her mind, Camryn would have never known that last night happened by looking at her car. She wasn't sure how Gino did it, but at the moment she didn't care. Camryn was just glad she didn't have to figure out how to tell Nana what happened.

Gino walked over to her and handed her the keys.

"I'm not saying thank you," Camryn said as she glared up at him.

"I don't need you to."

"Keep her away from me," Camryn said as tears threatened to fall from her eyes. Camryn's feelings for Gino hadn't left her heart, but her mind had been strong enough to know what wasn't good for her or her son.

"I will," Gino said before stepping a little closer to Camryn. He looked down towards her belly and smirked, "You take care of that baby."

Camryn looked up at him as he walked towards his truck. She bit her lip as a tear fell.

"Don't do it, Gino," she called after him. He stopped and turned towards her with a confused expression on his face. "Don't make me think you care."

Gino's nose flared as he slid into the driver's seat of his truck. Camryn glanced to see Baywood in the passenger seat before she locked her car door and went back into the house.

"You don't like him," Camryn spoke to her unborn son who had been doing flips and kicks the whole time they were near Gino. He settled down and Camryn sighed before locking the front door and going back into her room.

A painful expression graced Tameka's face as she slid down further into the soft pillows of Lori's couch. She violently tugged at her short un-weaved hair as her left hand attached itself to a bottle of Vodka. Lori frowned as she sat at her computer and scrolled through a listing of jobs.

"Meka, stop it, we can find something you're good at," Lori said. She was trying her best to reassure Tameka of a different future but Tameka was stuck in her own pity.

It had been three days since Gino and Tameka's fight and she had been at Lori's ever since.

Tameka was embarrassed at the fact that Lori had to get Gino off of her and she was hurt that he had put his hands on her to that extreme over his side chick. That night, Tameka realized that somewhere in time, she had become Gino's side chick, while Camryn had replaced her in Gino's heart.

The look in his eyes as he pulled Camryn out of the car had been an unwelcomed vision in Tameka's mind for days. He had fallen in love with this young girl and their child had only been a result of that love. Tameka knew that Gino would not admit it, but he didn't have to for it to be the truth.

One way or the other, Tameka had to get out. Lori told her that she needed a job of some sort to keep her mind off of her fall from the throne but after a while of searching, Tameka realized she had no skills. Tameka had graduated from high school and not even thought about college. She couldn't blame that on Gino because he had always asked her what she wanted to do. Tameka had always been content on playing his wife. She hadn't realized that all she was doing was playing.

"How about working at the bank," Lori said. Tameka frowned as she tipped the Vodka bottle to the ceiling and shook her head.

"I can't work at a bank."

"I'm through then," Lori said jumping up from the computer, "I'm not helping you if you keep shooting down every job I suggest."

Tameka glared at her best friend and sat up straight.

"Look at you, you think everything is good now that Chase is back. Sorry if I can't have a perfect man like yours. I just found out that my man is in love with someone else."

"First of all," Lori said cutting Tameka off, "Don't get mad at me because my man loves me. I have never thrown that in your face. And second of all, you didn't just find this out Tameka! You been knew! He's been messing with that girl for three years, your ass just didn't want to see it."

"Three years Lori?" Tameka asked feeling her heart break into another million pieces. Lori sighed.

"Look, you know I love you, but in my eyes, you can't be dumb anymore. You have to wake up and see that this man does not care about you, Tameka! It's time to get over it."

Tameka sighed as the front door open and Chase walked in. As always, Lori's smile was wide as she greeted her man before he could even close the front door. They kissed and loved on each other as Tia and Jacob ran past them and upstairs. They didn't even stop to hug Tameka like they usually did.

Tameka knew that Lori was right. Tameka knew that it was time to find something better than Gino but Tameka also knew that there was one thing stopping her. She had loved this man for half of her life. She was emotionally stuck to him and as long as he was breathing, Tameka knew he would have control over her. Tameka knew the power Gino had over her would not let her move on with her life.

Twan's words echoed in her mind. She had been Gino's bitch for too long. She had wasted the last few months trying to get revenge on the wrong person. It was time she made up for it.

"Girl you are getting so big," Mia said as she helped Cam off of the large steel steps as soon as the train came to a full stop. Cam rolled her eyes as Mia laughed, taking her duffle bag from her.

"Thanks, best friend," Cam said. Mia smiled before kissing Cam on her cheek.

It had been a week since the car accident and Cam had decided that no one would know about it unless they were there. She had a little over a month left of her pregnancy and didn't want to move until the baby was born. She had grown attached to her doctor and wanted her to deliver her son but after that, she and Nana were gone.

"So how was the ride?" Mia asked as she put Cam's things into the back seat of her car. Cam waited until they were driving out of the parking lot to tell her about the little girl that kept trying to poke her stomach. "Her mom didn't do anything?"

"No! She just let the little girl all in my personal space," Cam said. Mia laughed harder as she asked Cam if she had eaten. "I'm starving."

"Well, Jayson is cooking,"

"Nope."

"Come on Cam, he promised to be nice," Mia said wanting them to get along. "Plus, I have to work later and I'm not leaving you in my apartment alone."

"I can stay by myself for a few hours," Cam said crossing her arms above her belly. Mia pouted.

"Please, Cam I would feel so much better if you did. Just do it for me, pretty please?" Mia said.

Camryn fell victim to the innocent face Mia had given her and sighed.

"Fine, Mia," Camryn said defeated. "He just better not say anything stupid."

Mia squealed as she reassured Camryn that Jayson would be on his best behavior. Once they got to Mia's apartment, Camryn took a shower from being on the train so long. She and Mia talked a little before heading across the street to Jayson's apartment.

As soon as she opened Jayson's door, the aroma of meatloaf hit both of their noses and Camryn inhaled it while closing her eyes.

"I hope it tastes half as good as it smells," Camryn mumbled and Mia laughed telling her that it would be.

When they entered the kitchen, Camryn looked around and admired it. If she hadn't disliked Jayson, she would have complimented him on it.

"Hey Cousin," Mia said announcing to Jayson that they were there. He turned around and nodded.

"The food is just about done," he said, "How was the train ride?"

Camryn took a second to reply. She didn't expect him to ask and she half didn't expect him to say anything to her at all.

"It was okay," Camryn said, "But the smell of your food has my child doing flips."

They all laughed as Jayson told them to go ahead and sit down at the table.

Jayson placed a Caesar salad in the middle of his kitchen table before opening the oven and pulling out meatloaf.

The kitchen fell silent as the three ate.

"I hope you know that this will probably be gone before I leave," Cam said cutting her second piece of meatloaf.

"Just let me get some for work and you can knock yourself out."

Camryn nodded before she pulled a piece of the meat off with her fork and lifted it to her mouth. Mia laughed as Camryn closed her eyes and slowly chewed.

After they ate, Mia sat with Cam and Jayson for a little while until it was time for her to go to work. Jayson busied himself with his work. Cam didn't want to disturb him with the television so she pulled a book from her purse and curled up in the corner of his wrap around sofa.

Cam found herself dozing off until she heard Jayson silently curse. Part of her didn't want to talk to him but she saw no reason in sitting up in his house and not talking for hours on end. She curled the top corner of the page she was reading and closed the book before sitting up.

"What are you working on?" Cam asked. Jayson looked up at her before back at the book and sighed.

"This report my boss wants me to put together," he said. Camryn waited to see if he was going to say anything else and after a few minutes he didn't.

"What's it about?"

"The social ethics of the company," Jayson said turning a page.

"I love sociology," Camryn said, "But I thought Mia told me you were in public relations?"

"I am," Jayson said laughing. "That's why I'm struggling."

Camryn smiled before going to sit next to him. She gently rubbed her belly and he looked at her.

"I'm really good at this stuff, do you mind?" Camryn said pointing at the report. Jayson looked at her for a second then threw his hands up with a defeated smile. Camryn nodded before picking it up.

Jayson sat back and watched Camryn scan over the report.

"So he wants you to research the demographics of the office and relate them to this article?" Camryn asked looking back at Jayson. He narrowed his eyes and nodded. "Oh, I got this," Camryn said, adjusting herself on the couch. Jayson laughed as she sat back next to him.

"So, what you have to do is list all of the demographics."

"What are those?" Jayson asked. Camryn shook her head and smiled.

"Demographics are just the measures of diversity in the office. They can be gender, ethnicity, race, social status, things like that," Camryn said. "Did they give you that information?" Jayson nodded.

"He wants me to do the report and set up presentations for the office."

Camryn nodded as her and Jayson sat up and worked on his report. Camryn had to admit that it felt good to be working on something again. When she got her associate's she said she wouldn't go back to school, but working with Jayson on his project made her think about going to get her bachelor's in sociology.

"That's about it," Camryn said handing Jayson the pen. He put it down on his coffee table, stood up and bowed in front of her. Camryn rubbed her belly as she laughed and waved him off.

"You are a lifesaver," Jayson said. "I owe you girl."

"You know I will gladly take the rest of that meatloaf for payment."

They laughed as Jayson sat back down and looked at Camryn. She looked at him, looked down at her clothes and back at him.

"Is there something on me?" she asked. Jayson shook his head while licking his lips.

"No, you're good. I just pegged you wrong that's all," Jayson said. Camryn raised an eyebrow and smacked her lips.

"I bet, you were too busy judging what you thought you knew," Camryn said. Jayson nodded before throwing his hand up.

"I'm a man who admits when he's wrong," Jayson said grabbing Camryn's hand, "I apologize."

Camryn slowly slid her hand out of his.

"It's okay, I'm sure if I would have heard my story without knowing me I would think the same."

The two looked at each other for a second. The front door opened and Mia walked in with a smile on her face.

"Finally off of the clock," she said, closing the door behind her.

"I didn't realize it was that late," Camryn said, scooting away from Jayson a little. Mia looked at both of them and smirked.

"Are you ready?" Mia asked. Camryn nodded while getting her things together.

"Yes, I'm getting tired."

Mia sighed in content as she walked into the living room. Her shower was just what she needed to get the stresses from work from her mind. She smiled when she saw Camryn on the couch watching television.

"So what did you do while I was at work?" Mia asked as she sat on the couch across from Camryn. Camryn looked at Mia and smiled.

"Well, I kept eating," Cam said. Mia laughed. "And I helped him with his project for work."

Mia nodded, wondering if Jayson had asked Cam for help like she told him to or if Cam offered. Mia was glad that Cam had come to visit. She had missed her best friend something terrible. Although this was true, Mia had to admit that being away from Camryn made her realize some things about herself.

Growing up with Camryn, Mia always had someone to hide behind. She and Camryn did everything together. They had planned to go to school, have great careers, and get married. Mia was upset that Camryn had got involved with Gino. She felt Cam had messed up the whole plan. When Mia found out that Cam was pregnant and had been through so much drama with him, she felt bad for feeling that way.

Now Mia wanted to fix Cam's situation. She wanted to get her away from Gino and his mess. She had so much to worry about and Mia didn't think that Cam deserved all that drama. No matter how many warnings Cam ignored, she didn't deserve it.

"So what are we doing tomorrow?" Camryn asked.

"Well, Jayson has a studio session and then we are going to this Mexican restaurant that you are going to love."

"Studio session, he raps?" Cam asked. Mia shook her head.

"No, he sings," Mia said, smiling.

"Is he any good?"

"Girl yes," Mia said. "And I'm not just saying that because he's family."

They both laughed.

Gino watched as Baby sat two plates of food down on Twan's new kitchen table. She slid one in front of Gino and one in front of Twan. Twan smacked her on her backside before digging into his meal. Gino looked around a little more before raising his fork.

"You got this place laid out real quick," Gino said. Twan nodded before stuffing his face with macaroni and cheese.

"Bae, you want a beer or a soda?" Baby asked from the large stainless steel refrigerator.

"A beer, what you want G?"

"Let me get a soda," he said. Baby looked at them before nodding and reaching into refrigerator.

Baby sat the drinks in front of them and sat down next to Twan. She wasn't eating. Gino watched her lick her lips before her chinky eyes looked at Twan.

"So what's up, Gino?"

"Business is business," Gino said smiling. His money was the only thing he didn't have to worry about. Although he hadn't uncovered his snake, he wasn't seeing any shortages at the moment so he was good. He kept his eyes open. It was the only thing he could do with Tameka gone and Camryn out of town.

Gino was keeping tabs on Camryn for two reasons. He wasn't sure if Tameka was going to try something again and he wanted to make sure his seed was good. Gino knew that the baby Camryn was carrying was his. He knew he had her sprung to no end and she wouldn't cheat on him when they were messing around. He wasn't happy about having a baby, but it was coming.

"I'm not talking about business, I know that's good," Twan said putting his fork down and resting back in the chair. "You know Chase is trying to get Tameka out the crib. She's causing problems."

Gino shook his head and knew that Tameka was over there causing trouble with Lori and Chase. Gino didn't like Lori one bit but Chase was his boy and business partner. Tameka was being disrespectful and rude putting all these extra people in their business.

"Yeah, I'll go get her in a few days," Gino said, running his large hand down his face before focusing back on the plate in front of him. "This food is good girl," Gino said.

Baby's lips formed a slow grin. She nodded and told him thank you. Twan looked at her and bit his bottom lip.

While Gino ate, he looked around the kitchen in the new condo Twan had just purchased about 30 minutes away from their neighborhood, not too far from his own home. Gino was glad that his boy was beginning to get a taste of the finer things. He had been telling him to take advantage of their earnings for some time now. Although this was true, Gino wondered what brought about the change.

He figured it had to do with Baby. She and Twan had been dealing for a few months now and Gino felt he was moving a little fast with her. Gino was all for Twan getting love but he didn't want him to end up in the situation he was in.

"This is fly, home boy," Gino said, "How much garage space they give you?"

"Three spots," Twan said holding up the last three fingers on his right hand. Gino nodded in approval.

"Anyway, this good food had me forgetting why I came over," Gino said sitting up. "I'm thinking about going on vacation next week."

"That's what's up," Twan said and Baby nodded before getting up and walking out of the kitchen to leave the men to talk. "Where to?"

"Miami probably, somewhere nice," Gino said, "I need to chill for a couple days."

Twan laughed before nodding his head and taking a swig of his beer.

"Yeah, you definitely need to do that."

When drama unfolds in your life, it is always hard to see the obvious. You are so consumed with the big things that the little things slip right by you. You can never let your guard down because when you do, unexpected things happen, good or bad. We get too comfortable with our

decisions and our situations that we fail to see the
conditions of those around us. Yet we must always
remember when one door closes...

Baby pushed her elbow out of the car window and snapped her fingers to an old 2Pac song. She was in love with her new Benz, compliments of her new boo. Baby was living it up and loving Twan's attention. She had to admit that when she first became infatuated with him, she had no idea how much she would get caught up in him.

Twan's attitude had Baby gone. He was a strong man and she knew it would take a strong man to handle her. Once Twan figured out that Baby was really about him, it was on.

Baby felt that Twan had a lot of potential to be exactly what she needed. Baby wasn't about getting taken care of or scheming, she was an opportunist.

There was a time when Baby was dumb and naïve. She believed it was how she got her nickname from her family. She thought the best thing to have, was a man with money who could take care of her. She found out the hard way that life was not that simple. After a bad break up, Baby got herself together and began to love herself. She knew what she was capable of and went for it.

The song switched and Baby smiled while nodding her head a little harder.

Baby had been cruising through town, looking for something to get into. Twan had given her some ends to get them both some new clothes but she wasn't sure what mall she wanted to go to. She could go to the closest one but there stores were weak. She just wasn't sure if she felt like driving over half an hour to a good mall.

Baby ended up on Lori's street and smirked once she saw her, Tameka, and Tani on the porch while Lori's kids ran around the yard. Baby pulled over and parked, slid her shades on and hopped out of the car.

"Hey ladies," she said, strutting up the sidewalk in her black Jimmy Choo heels. The girls looked at her as she walked up and smiled.

"What's up, Baby," Tani said as Lori nodded but Tameka looked at the car.

"You driving a new whip?" Tameka asked. Baby looked from her new car back to Tameka and bit her lip.

"Well, my man does spoil me," Baby said, switching her purse to her other arm. "What you ladies up to today?"

"Trying to get this chick to go somewhere," Tani said pointing to Tameka. She had her hair spiked up in a short cut but she wasn't dressed how she usually was whenever Baby saw her. She had on a plain blue shirt with some jeans and sneakers. Baby looked Tameka over and wondered how someone could lose themselves over a man.

"You should hit up the mall with me," Baby said looking at Tameka. She looked up at her but just shook her head. "Come on girl, I've never seen you looking like this."

"You just started seeing me a few months ago," Tameka said.

"No, I've been with Twan for a few months, I've been seeing you. You letting this dude get to your head, you think he's walking around mopping?" Baby asked. Lori and Tani both agreed with Baby.

"What would you know about how I feel?"

Baby smirked before remembering when she almost had been like Tameka. She was 18 at the time. Her boyfriend of several years tried to play her and ended up putting his hands on her. The whole city would talk about what Baby did to him and how it was his last time putting his hands on anybody.

"I know that if you give someone all your power, he'll take it," Baby said with a serious face. "I let someone get me like that but I got him back. You always get them back."

"Oh snap, I remember that," Tani said loudly, making Baby glare at her. "Didn't you try to slice some dude up a few years back?"

"He tried me. I tried to kill him," Baby said, almost proud of what she had done. "He's lucky his boy stopped me. All I'm saying Tameka is, G is on a high horse and he needs to be brought down."

Tameka looked over Baby and slowly nodded.

"So are you riding with me or what?"

"Let me go change."

It was Cam's last night visiting Mia and she found herself back in Jayson's apartment while Mia was at work. Cam was wondering if Mia had planned this all along. Cam had to admit that ever since Jayson and she had been civil to each other, she didn't mind spending time at his place.

It didn't hurt that he always cooked some wonderful meal for her either. Tonight it was steak, baked sweet potatoes, and macaroni and cheese.

"I definitely have to have some of this for the train ride home," Cam said pouring cinnamon over the melted butter on her sweet potato. Jayson nodded while taking a bite of his steak.

"My doctor is going to flip because I know I've probably gained some weight up here with you."

"The kid is happy though, right?" Jayson asked. Cam smiled.

"Yes, he is."

After the two ate, Cam caught up on her book while Jayson worked out in his room.

Even though she was alone, Cam couldn't help that her thoughts were distracting her reading. Cam was sure that Gino would keep his word by keeping Tameka away from her, but what would happen after she had the baby? Was her son never going to know his father? If Gino stayed with Tameka, could Cam trust her around her son? Even if she did trust them, would she let them see her son anyway?

Cam smirked as the baby kicked, obviously reading her thoughts. She felt so in tune with her son. She couldn't wait to see him. She just prayed that she could protect him after his birth just as well as she had while he was in the womb.

Cam looked towards the door frame that led to Jayson's bedroom. She could hear his weights clanking together for about an hour and half before they stopped.

A shirtless, perspiring Jayson walked around the corner and leaned against the frame. He wiped his face with a small black towel before smiling at Cam. She forced herself to stop looking at his chest and focus on his face.

"You alright in here?" Jayson asked and Cam nodded. "Well, I'm about to take a shower, you need to use the bathroom before I get in there?"

"No," Cam said looking back down at her book,."I'm good."

Jayson looked at her for a second before nodding and disappearing behind the corner.

Cam bit her lip as she tried to focus back on her book. She couldn't explain the feeling that suddenly rushed over her. It excited her but at the same time, scared her to death. She liked Jayson and didn't know how to deal with it.

Although she had already talked to her this morning, Cam had the urge to call Nana. She decided against it seeing that it was going on ten and knew that Nana was sleeping. So Cam was left to deal with her feelings on her own.

It had been a while since she experienced the initial attraction a woman has with a man. Almost four years ago when she met Gino was the last time. She had been so consumed with him that no other man could steal her attention.

Jayson was the first man she was attracted to after Gino and that scared her even more. Surely Jayson wasn't Gino, but how was she to know that. Would he even want to talk to someone in her situation? She could honestly say that she wouldn't if it was vice versa. Camryn wasn't even sure if she should be feeling the way she was feeling being two months away from having a baby.

Cam laughed at herself before turning back to her book, only to be interrupted by the one who had consumed her thoughts for the past hour.

Jayson came in, now wearing some basketball shorts and a baggy tee shirt, and sat next to Cam on the couch.

"I would have thought you would have been sleep by now," he joked. Cam tried to smile, but before she could respond Jayson snatched the book out of her hand. He slid his hand onto the page Cam was on and closed the book over it, not to lose her spot. He read over the cover before looking at her. "Is this any good?"

"So far," Cam said shifting her position as her son moved around. "Stephanie Perry Moore is my favorite author."

"What, does she write those man bashing books?" Jayson asked laughing. Cam snatched the book back and giggled.

"No, she's actually a Christian fiction writer, one of the realest I've read too." Cam said. Jayson nodded.

Cam got caught up in his glance of her and felt her throat get dry. She was almost sure there was a connection, some type of attraction between the two but she wouldn't chance it by assuming. She had to know.

"Can I ask you a question?" she said, surprising herself with what she wanted to ask. Jayson nodded quickly before saying she could ask him anything. "Are you attracted to me?"

Jayson smirked and Camryn immediately threw her hand up.

"I mean I was just wondering. I know I'm not in the best position to be asking," Cam said with her hand on her stomach. "I'm sorry, but I just felt something and wanted to know, if..."

Jayson slid his hand over the one that lay on Cam's stomach and hushed her.

"Camryn, don't apologize for asking a question. You don't know until you ask," Jayson said but Cam waited silently for her answer.

"Despite your situation and our first impressions of each other, yes, I am attracted to you."

Camryn smiled, that was all she needed at the moment.

Gino slid up and down the three levels of the mall buying Tameka new clothes, shoes and jewelry. He had dropped at least eight hundred so far and made three trips back to the truck to put some bags up. He had stopped by her beauty salon before going to the mall and given them three hundred dollars to put micros in her hair and do her nails and feet. He had Chase tell Lori to drop her off there and the salon would call him once she was done.

Gino was bringing Tameka home tonight.

He had thought it over and realized that Camryn was out of his life. He was sure she wouldn't let him anywhere near his son. Tameka had always been there for him and he had done her wrong. He disrespected her and he knew that was what had her acting crazy. He planned on making it up to her.

Gino passed Jared's Jewelry and backed up into it. When the clerk saw how many bags he had in his hand, she immediately greeted him with a smile.

"I'm looking for a tanzanite and diamond ring in white gold, preferably over a carat of princess cut diamonds," Gino said as the clerk led him over to the tanzanite section.

"I see you know your jewelry," the woman said smiling as she looked through the glass before pulling out a row of rings similar to what Gino had told her.

"That one," Gino pointed to the one on the end. It had an oval shaped pure tanzanite in the middle and each side had a cluster of three diamonds. "Give me the stats." Gino said, sitting at the stool in front of the counter.

"This is a LeVian piece, if you are familiar with him you know that he uses only the purest grades and cuts of all stones. Each side holds 1.25 carat diamonds which equals 2.50 carat altogether. The band is 14 carat white gold."

Gino knew that tanzanite was Tameka's favorite stone. It was time she got one of the things she asked for.

"If you have it in a size 7, wrap it up,"

The clerk immediately grabbed one of the leather boxes under the counter before putting the ring into the cleaner while she rang it up.

"Is this for a special occasion?" she asked as Gino pulled out crisp 100-dollar bills from his pocket. He counted 30 of them before placing them on the counter and nodding.

"A proposal, perhaps."

"You're man must love you."

Tameka didn't respond as the girl applied moose to her fresh braids. The tingle felt good. Tameka was glad to have gotten her hair done. She had to admit that she knew Gino was going to go all out to get her home, but she just wasn't sure how she would handle it.

Tameka didn't feel love for Gino anymore. She loved him for so many years and her love was always degraded and disrespected. She had learned to play her role though. She would play it off and see what he had up his sleeve, but she wasn't through torturing him. He hadn't even begun to feel the pain she felt. She was going to make him feel it.

Tameka heard the girl that was doing her hair call Gino to let him know that she was done with Tameka's braids. Another girl began to wax her eyebrows as someone else sprayed her nails with quick dry.

Tameka was back in her element and it felt great.

When she went shopping with Baby, she realized that she and Camryn weren't that different from each other. She even felt sorry for her that she ended up pregnant by Gino. Tameka was glad that all those years of wanting to have his baby didn't pay off.

Baby's "get even" motto had stuck with Tameka. She smiled as devious plans raced through her mind. She had to admit that she was happy to be leaving Lori's house. She loved her best friend and the kids but living with them was horrible. Especially since her and Chase were always hugged up every chance they got.

Tameka slid her hands into the nail dryer just to make sure they were fully dry. She hadn't been sitting for more than five minutes before Gino's truck pulled up. Tameka bit her lip as he came into view. She hadn't seen him in over a month. He had a fresh haircut, his jewelry was shining, and his outfit was just right for the occasion.

He had on some dark denim jeans, a black beater that showed off his tattooed muscles and some black and white Jordan's. Tameka couldn't see his eyes because his black and white NY hat was pulled over them.

The bell went off as he entered the salon. Tameka didn't move but she followed him with her eyes as he asked the girl at the counter if he had given her enough to cover everything earlier. She giggled and told him yes. Tameka rolled her eyes.

Gino spotted her and made his way over to her just as she pulled her hands from under the dryer. He smiled before pulling her up by her elbow and wrapping his arms around her. Tameka's heart sped up as he lifted her chin to kiss her.

"How you feeling?" he whispered against her lips.

"I'm good," Tameka said. He nodded before pulling her purse around her shoulder and leading her out of the shop. He opened the door to the truck for her and closed it. Tameka looked at all the bags in the backseat from her favorite stores and smirked as Gino got in the car.

"You hungry?" Gino asked. Tameka nodded.

Gino took Tameka out to eat before they finally got home. Being away for so long, Tameka walked around for a minute. She had to admit that she missed her home. She had rightfully earned her place there.

She looked through some of the bags Gino had before putting her things up. Her closet was full of new clothes and shoes and she loved it. Now that the old

Tameka was back with a new attitude, she needed new clothes.

Tameka slipped into some shorts and a beater as she waited for Gino to get out of the shower.

While waiting, she soon went to sleep.

Tameka felt a tap on her thigh and it caused her to wake up. When she opened her eyes, Gino was sitting next to her on the bed with his hands behind his back.

"Sit up for me," Gino said. Tameka yawned before slowly pushing herself up.

"What else you got?" Tameka asked smiling knowing that her gifting wasn't over.

"You know I love you right?" Gino said which took Tameka by surprise. "You are the only female I would do all this shit for you know?"

"I know," Tameka said with a smirk on her face. She wasn't sure that equaled love at all. She began to say something but when Gino revealed what was in his hands, Tameka was speechless.

"I know it's tight between us right now but it's always been me and you against the world. I disrespected you and that was wrong but we have to get over the past and live for now." Gino opened the box and Tameka's hand flew to her mouth as the ring came into view. "I'm ready to flip your name, Meka."

Tameka began to cry as she jumped on Gino, kissing all over his face before he could even put the ring on.

Camryn groaned as she wondered how she ended up lying in bed on her back. She really had to pee and she couldn't figure out how to roll around to get out of bed.

"You are really big, son," Camryn said as she slid her hand around the post and pulled herself up. Once she gained her balance she hurried to the bathroom and swung the door open. She sighed in relief as she used the bathroom for what seemed like ten minutes.

When Camryn finally got back into her room, she saw that her phone was flipped open and a call was still on. She laughed as she read the time and the name before picking it up.

"Jayson," she said as she heard him breathing, "Jayson, wake up!" she yelled.

"What?" he asked. Camryn laughed before telling him that they had fallen asleep on the phone. "I wasn't sleep,"

"Yes you were, hang up and go back to sleep," Camryn said. Jayson groaned something before hanging up and Camryn laughed as she did the same.

It had been about two weeks since she came from Mia's school and her and Jayson had spent hours at a time on the phone ever since. They hadn't spoken much about their mutual attraction but Camryn was content.

She liked that she could talk to Jayson without feeling like he would think a certain way about her. She was able to confide in him and now that he knew the whole story with Gino, Jayson apologized to Camryn for how he acted with her when they first met. Camryn was over it and glad to have another friend besides Mia to talk to.

Noting that her son was up and flipping around, Camryn knew that her thoughts of lying back down and sleeping all day would not work.

Camryn took a shower and threw on some red leggings and a long, oversized black tank dress. She had been extremely hot even though it was nearing November and since she wasn't going anywhere, she figured her attire would do for the day.

Camryn began to make lunch for her and Nana when her cell phone rang. She smiled seeing Jayson's name pop up.

"Hey sleepy head," she said.

"My phone was burning my face when I woke up," he said. Camryn laughed.

"I told you to hang up."

"What are you doing," Jayson said, ignoring her last statement.

"Cooking grilled chicken for me and Nana's Caesar salad."

"You never cooked for me while you were here," Jayson said.

"You did all the cooking, I didn't need to."

The whole time they talked, Camryn couldn't erase the smile from her face. She had butterflies in her stomach and they were intensified when she realized that the feeling was totally different from how she felt with Gino in the beginning.

Getting to know Jayson proved that he was so much more than she thought. She had always been attracted to Gino because of his strength and how people looked at him. With Jayson, he was more like her. He had a sense of humor, he showed a genuine interest in her life and he wasn't afraid to admit his faults and mistakes.

"Has your mail come yet," Jayson asked. Camryn frowned as she began cutting up the grilled chicken to put in the salad.

"No, why?"

"Just wondering," Jayson said.

"Jayson, what did you do?" Camryn asked with a smile on her face.

"I don't know what you're talking about," Jayson said and Camryn laughed at how he was acting. "But you should eat and call me back when your mail comes," he said.

"Okay."

After they hung up, Camryn took the salads and something to drink into Nana's room and they ate in there while Nana read the Bible to her and the baby.

When the doorbell rang, they both looked out the window to see the Edible Arrangements truck outside. Camryn smiled as she got up and went to the front door.

"Camryn Lacey?" the woman asked and Camryn nodded before signing the form. She couldn't help but smile at the beautiful arrangement of fruits shaped as flowers. Once she got it in the kitchen, she pulled one of the apples dipped in chocolate out while opening the card.

"Tribute to a woman," Camryn read aloud. "If I had a star, I would name it after your smile. It could never outshine you, but it would represent your being. I've apologized for misunderstanding you, but now I must apologize for everyone else in the world, who does not see you for what you are."

Camryn bit her finger as she tried not to cry. She wouldn't admit it then, but in just a few sentences, Jayson had won her heart.

Camryn took the arrangement and the card into Nana's room. Nana read it to herself while Camryn picked up her cell phone to call Jayson.

Mind Games

Tameka held her left hand out with her fingers spread, showing off her engagement ring. Tani grabbed her hand as Lori leaned over to look as well.

"Girl this rock is fat," Tani said trying to take it off of Tameka's finger to try it on. Tameka smacked her hand back and closed her fist so that Tani couldn't get it off. It had been almost a week since Gino proposed and Tameka hasn't let the ring out of her sight.

"So we're going to the Bahamas in two weeks to do it," Tameka said smiling from ear to ear. Lori frowned.

"Two weeks?"

"Yeah, and G flying you, Chase, and the kids out to be the witnesses," Tameka said. Tani commented on why she couldn't go but no one responded.

"Don't you think two weeks is a little too soon, Meka?" Lori said. Tameka frowned.

"I've been waiting on this seven years so no, two weeks is not too soon."

Lori shut up, knowing that convincing Tameka otherwise would be impossible.

Tameka twirled her ponytail of micro braids around and told Tani and Lori what she planned to wear.

"Anyway, are we still going to the Kid Bounce tomorrow for the twin's birthday?" Tameka asked, finally tired of talking about her wedding plans.

"Yeah, it starts at 2," Lori said rubbing her hardened belly. She had found out a few weeks ago that she was three months pregnant. She hadn't wanted to tell Tameka but ever since she got engaged to Gino, she had been in a good mood. She took the news a lot better than Lori thought. She was even excited to be an aunt again.

"Should she even been on a plane to the Bahamas?" Tani asked pointing to Lori. Lori rolled her eyes as Tameka waved her off.

"She'll be fine, it's first class she'll have plenty of room to move around."

"Yeah, you don't need to worry about me," Lori said. Tani began to say something but Tameka reminded them that Gino was upstairs sleeping before they started arguing.

"Nobody cares," Tani said, getting up and grabbing her things. Lori and Tameka just watched as she left.

"Bitter bitch," Lori mumbled. Tameka hit her in her arm and laughed. "What, she is!"

"So what," Tameka said sitting back, shoulder to shoulder with Lori.

"But for real, Meka," Lori said turning her head towards her. "I know you're all excited about the wedding and I'm happy for you, but are you sure about this?"

Tameka looked at Lori and shook her head. Of course, everyone thought she was dumb, some even thought Gino didn't love her. Why would he marry her if he didn't? Tameka knew it looked as if she was making a big mistake, but she knew better.

"Trust me, Lori. I know what I'm going."

Gino woke up to the sounds of Tameka saying bye to Lori and cooking in the kitchen. He had to admit that he wasn't sure about the whole marriage thing, but ever since he'd asked Tameka, she had been everything he wanted.

Gino took his time showering and doing his usual hygiene but only put on some boxers, basketball shorts and socks. When he made his way down to the kitchen, he smiled at the sight of Tameka's body in some dark gray sweat pants, rolled up her calves, and a red sports bra. She had music playing on the television in the kitchen and her braids were pulled up into a high ponytail. She was working her hips in a little dance while manning the stove.

She froze when she felt Gino's strong arms around her, but smiled when she realized what was going on.

"I was trying to finish before you got up," Tameka said turning just as Gino kissed her cheek. He smiled as he looked down at her shining ring. She had cleaned it every day since he gave it to her. Gino kissed Tameka's neck and smiled.

"What is that I smell?" he asked with a knowing smirk. Tameka giggled before pulling a blunt from her other ear and putting it in Gino's face. Gino inhaled the scent before wrapping his hand around it. He gripped Tameka's waist with his right hand as he turned her so that he could kiss her.

As he was walking to the table to get a lighter, he smirked.

"*I should have given her a ring a long time ago,*" Gino thought to himself.

Gino smoked his blunt and ate as soon as Tameka was done with the food. She sat and talked to Baby on the phone while filing her nails. Gino thought it was a little weird that her and Baby had become such good friends considering that Tameka only really hung with Lori or Tani. Gino shrugged it off.

"Do you need anything from the store before we go?" Gino asked. "I need to get some clothes and shoes."

"I got enough new stuff," Tameka said.

"That's new stuff for here, not the Bahamas," Gino said smiling. Tameka told Baby she would call her back before closing her phone and looking at Gino.

"Whatever you say," she said smiling before picking his empty plate up from in front of him. "You're the boss."

Gino smiled as Tameka walked away from him towards the kitchen sink.

After his high wore off, Gino began to make calls to Twan, Baywood, and a few others. He knew this vacation was well needed but he also knew that he had a lot of things to get in order before he left.

"We have a problem," Baywood said when Gino called him.

"What is it now?" Gino said, the stresses of his empire falling on his shoulders like a weight.

"It seems our snake isn't dead, this money count from last month is not what it should be."

"Who counted Afton or Jay," Gino said ready to get to the bottom of this.

"All three of us did," Baywood said, "I don't let anybody count in here if I'm not here."

Gino respected what Baywood did but now he had an even bigger problem. He only had about four days to get things under control. He knew that Tameka would kill him if the trip was delayed or cancelled so that was out.

"G," Baywood said snapping Gino out of his thoughts, "Man, don't worry about it you got home to worry about, let us focus on this."

Gino hated leaving the fate of his business in the hands of someone else. A week away could do a lot of damage to his empire.

"If we find out anything, I'll keep you posted. If I catch this cat while you're gone,"

"Leave him for me," Gino said finishing Baywood's sentence.

"No problem."

A few days later and they were on their way to marriage.

Tameka's mind was racing. She had waited so long for this that it seemed she had tunnel vision. After all the things that Gino put her through, her focus was solely on becoming his wife.

She pushed her toes into the green, plush grounding of the gondola that resembled grass as the clergyman began to recite from the small, dark red book in his hand. She could hear Lori behind her whispering to Tia to be still. She could hear the waves crashing against the shore behind the gondola and birds in the distance calling to each other. She had never been at peace like this before.

"I require and charge you both, as you stand in the presence of God, before whom the secrets of all hearts are disclosed, that, having duly considered the holy covenant you are about to make, you do now declare before this company your pledge of faith, each to the other."

Tameka wasn't sure what all of his words meant, so she just smiled. She glanced at her right to see her man standing tall. He looked towards her and winked.

"Will you please face each other and hold hands," the clergyman commanded while waving his hand between the two. Tameka shifted before turning to face Gino. Gino gripped her hands before looking up at her. She never saw this coming. Granted, she always wanted it but never saw Gino committed that officially to her. No rings and no kids he would always say.

The clergyman turned slightly towards Gino and nodded.

"Gino Watson, wilt thou have this woman to be thy wedded wife, to live together in the holy bonds of matrimony? Wilt thou love her, comfort her, honor and keep her, in sickness and in health; and forsaking all others, keep thee only unto her so long as ye both shall live?"

"Yeah," Gino said. Tameka's face dropped as Chase laughed behind the. The clergyman even smiled but Tameka saw nothing funny.

"The correct term is I do," he said. Gino's nose flared slightly and he rolled his eyes.

"My fault, I do."

Tameka had almost forgotten what a bastard he could be. She had been blinded by the superficial notion that becoming his wife would make everything better. That somehow that small ring and piece of paper saying her name had changed would make all of their issues disappear, that the chilling effect on her heart would reverse.

It hadn't.

"Tameka Skanes, wilt thou have this man to be thy wedded husband, to live together in the holy bonds of matrimony? Wilt thou love him, comfort him, honor and keep him, in sickness and in health; and forsaking all others, keep thee only unto him so long as ye both shall live?"

Tameka loved him for so long. She always put him above herself. When he was hurt or sick she nursed him. When he was upset she did everything she could to help.

Tameka had even helped build his empire. She had done all these vows and more but what had she gotten?

Something as simple as him saying the wrong words at their wedding knocked her back into the reality of things.

She was no longer concerned with Gino's wellbeing. It was time for her to step up and be a new Tameka. With revenge in her eyes, she smiled.

"I do."

Gino smiled at her as the clergyman continued on.

"Since you have already promised each other to live together in marriage and have now openly witnessed the same before God and this company, and have declared the same by joining of hands, I now pronounce you to be man and wife before God."

A kiss sealed the deal as Chase, Lori, and the kids began to clap and congratulate them. Once the clergyman dismissed them from the gondola, Lori hugged her best friend and kissed her cheek.

"As long as you're happy, I'm good," Lori said with worry in her eyes. Tameka rubbed Lori's belly before glancing at Gino, who was walking towards her with Chase and Jacob.

"I will be."

"I think you'll go early," Nana said as she smoothed the thick cocoa butter over Camryn's stomach as they rested on the couch. Camryn frowned.

"Nana, what makes you say that?" Camryn asked.

"You're stomach has dropped," Nana said. Camryn looked down and noticed that her stomach was a little lower than it had been.

"It'd be awesome if he came on the first," Camryn said and Nana smiled, "I hear the first baby of the year gets everything."

They both laughed. Nana asked when Mia was coming home since it was the end of November.

"She'll be home on the 15," Camryn said before she bit her lip, "Her, her aunt and Jayson are coming,"

Nana smiled.

"Does he want you to meet his mom?" Nana asked and Camryn nodded.

"I don't know if I should," Camryn said as she continued to rub the cocoa butter in.

"Why child?"

"Nana I'm seven months pregnant, Jayson doesn't need that mess. I don't want to risk Gino or anyone seeing him with me. I don't want to drag him into this," Camryn said as she realized she had deep feelings for Jayson. She would blame herself if anything happened to him.

"Baby, you got pregnant seven months ago, a lot of things can change in seven months. He's not asking you to run away with him, Camryn," Nana said laughing.

"I know."

"And you'd probably meet her anyway eventually through Mia," Nana stated. Camryn looked at her and nodded.

"It's about time for me to get ready for Bible study," Nana said pushing herself off of the couch. Camryn put her feet down on the floor and got prepared to get up.

"And you weren't going to tell me?"

"I didn't think you wanted to go," Nana said as she laughed a little at Camryn struggling to get off the couch.

"You don't love me," Camryn joked as she went into her room to get ready.

For the last month or so, Camryn had been going to church with Nana almost every time she went. It didn't matter if it was Bible study, morning worship or Sunday school, Camryn wanted to go. She felt safe there and she always learned something new. It had even surprised her that she and Jayson had been having conversations regarding the Bible. They would get into conversations about certain stories that they knew in common and talk about them for hours.

"Looks like I talked you up," Camryn said to herself as she looked at her phone ringing, flashing Jayson's name across the screen. After she slid on her Ugg boots, she sat down on her bed and hit talk.

"What are you doing?" Camryn asked.

"I'm trying to get my Moms situated since she's coming early."

"Really?" Camryn said getting nervous once again.

"Yeah, I wouldn't be surprised if you met that nosy woman before Mia and I get there."

"Are you serious?"

"Ryn, calm down, she's not going to kill you," Jayson said and Camryn rolled her eyes at herself for being so nervous. "She's just anxious to meet you."

"You've been talking about me?" Camryn asked with a smile.

"Maybe."

"Camryn Charmaine, are you ready?" Nana called from the hallway.

"Yes ma'am," Camryn called back before pushing herself off the bed. "I'll call you later."

The limo pulled up at Gino and Tameka's home to end their wedding vacation. Tameka ran her manicured nails down Gino's neck to see how she was going to wake him up. He had slept almost the whole ride from the airport but Tameka wasn't surprised.

Tameka tried to lift Gino up off of her chest by pushing her body off the leather seat. He groaned and pushed his weight back down on her, causing her back to hit the seat. Tameka ran her tongue over her teeth and smiled.

"We're home, boo," Tameka said. Gino lazily threw his arms around Tameka's shoulders.

"Carry me," he said. Tameka laughed as the driver opened the door.

"Yeah right G, get up," Tameka said. The driver smiled at the newlyweds as Gino finally sat up and got himself together. He pulled two bills out of his pocket and gave them to the driver. The driver nodded quickly with a smile before he began unloading the trunk with all of their things. Gino had almost as many suitcases as Tameka did, if not more.

It was as if the hood had radar on Gino and knew he was home. His cell phone began to ring as soon as Tameka entered the alarm code in the foyer.

Tameka listened to Gino instruct Baywood on some things. He said something about just getting home and had better things to do than run from spot to spot. He asked where Twan was and what was going on with what he told them before he left.

While Tameka was in Gino's walk in closet, she remained close to the entrance so that she could hear. Gino had gotten quiet but Tameka knew she heard him mention Camryn's name. Tameka shook her head at even thinking that he still hadn't been keeping tabs on her. After what she had done to her, she expected him to. She wasn't stupid and in fact, she had planned on talking to Camryn anyway.

Now that she was married to Gino and Camryn was still having his son, Tameka felt that Camryn deserved some type of help. She knew Gino wouldn't do it willingly, so Tameka wanted to make sure he did it anyway.

She knew that no one would believe that she wanted to help Camryn. Truth of the matter was Tameka was no longer envious of her. Tameka could only imagine what it would have been like to get pregnant by a man who was insanely against having a seed. All the things she had heard Gino had done to that poor girl and she was about to be stuck raising a kid by herself.

Tameka unpacked the rest of their things before Gino was off the phone.

She leaned against the dresser and watched as Gino flopped down on the bed. She smirked before walking over to him and straddling his waist. Gino instinctively gripped her hips.

"I was thinking," Tameka said massaging Gino's shoulders, "How about I make some runs for you today," she said. Gino opened his eyes and looked at her.

"My husband has been working so hard and he never gets to rest, I just want you to relax and enjoy your day," Tameka said kissing on Gino's neck. "It'll be just like old times and then I'll come home and cook for you and then give you a massage and roll you a big, fat blunt. How does that sound?"

"Sounds like you're trying to butter me up for something," Gino said with a smile, pulling Tameka down to kiss her. She swung her left hand around to look at her ring.

"Oh, I got just what I want," she said. "Tell me what you need me to do."

"Go to the spot on Manchester and tell Afton to give you the drop for tomorrow. It should be in two bags, bring one here and take one to Twan's." Tameka nodded, taking mental notes. "Don't be all day Tameka, make sure you go to Manchester first. Jay might have you run some work to Baywood but get the money first."

Tameka nodded before leaning down to kiss Gino telling him she would handle it all.

"*I have some runs to make too,*" Tameka said to herself.

How quickly we forget how we've hurt someone. We see them changing their ways and we never ever stop to think that they've harbored negative feelings and the hurtful things you've done to them just go away. What we fail to realize is that years and years of lies, deceit, hatred, pain and depression don't just go away.

Baby rolled her eyes as she listened to one of Twan's customers run her mouth about how she didn't have the money for what she was asking for. Baby sucked her teeth as she crossed her long legs and straightened her back. She pushed herself against the stairs and tapped her fingernails against each other.

"So this is how we'll handle this little situation," Baby said. The woman shut up. "Either you have the money for what you're asking for, or you're leaving, still breathing and thankful because you don't have the money and you're wasting my time," Baby said pulling her shades off so she could see the woman walk away with her head down. Baby smirked before Gino's truck pulled up in the driveway took over her attention.

When Baby saw Tameka strutting around the car, she smiled.

"What's good, Mrs. G," Baby said standing up and moving over on the staircase. Tameka nodded with a smile, pulling her dark brown Chanel shades from over her eyes.

"Twan has you working Baby?" Tameka asked as she knocked on the wooden door three times.

"No mami, Baby is supervising," she said. Tameka laughed a little before Jay finally opened the door.

"I know you knew that I was coming, what took so long to get the door?" Tameka asked as she pushed him aside and her and Baby walked in. Jay blinked slowly before closing the door.

"Hi to you, too," Jay said. Tameka gave him a fake smile and asked where Afton was. "He just ran to the store up the street," Jay said sitting back down in front of the television that was plastered on the wall.

"Seriously, I know G called and said I was on my way," Tameka said sitting down next to Baby, who sat on the couch opposite of Jay.

"Chill out boss lady," Jay joked. They all laughed. Baby glanced at Tameka to see her smiling a little too hard. She could tell she liked the sound of boss lady.

"So boss lady," Baby said dragging out her words, "How was the trip?"

"It was so fly," Tameka said smiling. "I can't say that I'm glad to be home."

"What is G doing?"

"Oh, I told him I would handle his business today," Tameka said waving her hand. Baby raised an eyebrow as Afton came in the room and asked Jay to help him split up some work so Tameka could take it to Twan when she dropped the money off with him.

"He lets you do that?" Baby asked. Jay smirked at Baby's question before walking out of the room following Afton.

"Girl, who you think helped him do all this? Yeah Baywood and Twan were there but I put in lots of work for this empire," Tameka boasted on her devotion and loyalty to Gino. Baby nodded, realizing that she hadn't put enough stock in Tameka as she should have.

Baby knew she needed to re-evaluate her plans after learning that Tameka knew more about the business than she had appeared to.

"Meka, we're almost done and Baywood expects you in the next twenty minutes," Afton said from the back room. Tameka and Baby both nodded, Baby knew that the drive between spots was strategically placed in short distance from each other so that if the runner did not get to one or the other in a specific amount of time, they knew something was wrong. Baby was sure that Tameka knew all of this.

"So, our party is tomorrow night right?" Tameka asked Baby who only nodded. Twan was throwing Gino and Tameka a party at one of the clubs downtown in the VIP lounge, since none of them were able to celebrate when the actual wedding was. Tameka was excited.

"Yeah, I hope your fit is fly," Baby said and Tameka laughed.

"I'm going to pick up a few things after I run our errands," Tameka said. Baby caught on to her saying our instead of his. She just nodded.

"Well, I actually need to get home to my man," Baby said standing up, "I'll see you tomorrow night."

They said their byes and Baby went out the back door towards her car. She smiled at her interaction with Tameka as the wheels in her head began to turn. Baby had an even better plan.

Mia sighed as she finished packing the clothes she would need for her visit home. She had to pack an extra bag just for the things she bought for her Godson. Mia had been spending all of her free money on the baby and he wasn't even here yet.

Mia was very excited to go home for Christmas break. She had three weeks off of school and she would be home when Camryn had the baby. She couldn't wait to move around and not worry about classes, but there was one downfall to going home.

His name was Jeremiah. He had the prettiest smile and was one of the smartest guys Mia had ever met. They had become friends through the minority student organization they were both in and Mia could almost say she was in love. Jeremiah was in his third year at the university. They weren't officially together, but they had been dating for a few months.

Mia had to admit that besides Jayson, if it hadn't been for Jeremiah she probably wouldn't have made it through the semester. Even though she was 20, she had always been under her mom and Camryn. She wasn't used to doing things on her own or making decisions for herself. Jeremiah helped her through that and she learned how to be more independent.

The one she thought of pulled up outside of her apartment and she rushed to her front door to let him in. He wasn't so excited about her going home for the break since he was staying around campus. Mia didn't want him to be upset so he told her that to show her that he wasn't, he was coming over to cook dinner for her before she left.

"What's up," Jeremiah said with a smile. Mia smiled at him while helping carry the bags of groceries he bought up the stairs. Once they put the bags down on the table, Jeremiah turned to Mia and rubbed his hands together.

"Now where is my proper greeting," he said. Mia smiled hard before walking into his open arms and hugging him. He pulled away slightly to give her a kiss. Every time he kissed her, Mia blushed. She lingered on his lips a second before sighing. He went over to wash his hands after they parted.

"Do you need any help?" Mia asked peeking into one of the bags. Jeremiah swatted her hand away, she grabbed it with her other hand and smiled.

"No, you chill out and let me do this," he said. Mia nodded and made her way out of the kitchen.

Mia moaned as she slid her fork out of her mouth, leaving no traces of the chicken parmesan that Jeremiah had prepared. Jeremiah almost had Jayson on his cooking skills but since Jayson learned from her mom and their grandmother, no one could touch him except those two and Nana.

"That's it, I'm staying," Mia joked. Jeremiah laughed.

"I wish it was that easy," he said. Mia frowned a little before smiling.

"I'll only be gone for three weeks or so," Mia said patting his hand from across the table. Jeremiah licked his lips before putting his fork down and looking at Mia. She looked down and began to get nervous. The way he was looking at her was making her a little uncomfortable. "Jeremiah, I'll be back before you know it."

"When you come back I want an answer," he said. Mia sighed.

Jeremiah had asked her a few days ago to be his woman. It would have been all fine until he explained exactly what he was looking for. Jeremiah wasn't that much older but he wasn't into casual dating. He explained to Mia that he didn't want his attention to her to go unnoticed. Jeremiah wanted a serious relationship. He had taken the time to get to know Mia and once he was satisfied with what he found out, he wanted her to be his woman. He wasn't asking Mia to marry him, but he did express to her his need to know he had someone he could trust and eventually love. Jeremiah knew he could spend hours with Mia doing nothing and not be bored. He was ready to see if they could work on a long-term status.

Mia hadn't answered him yet because she was terrified. Jeremiah wasn't rushing her.

Mia had never been in a serious relationship, or any relationship for that matter. In fact, she was still a virgin. All of her life, Mia had been focusing on her school work and church and hardly partied. The few times she did go out it was when Camryn would drag her somewhere. After seeing everything that Cam went through with Gino, Mia was scared to go down that road of love that so many fell crazy on. Mia had made a decision to not have sex before marriage. She didn't want to change her morals because someone's charm.

So far, Jeremiah seemed to be respectful of her wishes but Mia wanted to be sure she was ready for all he wanted.

"Is that fair?" Jeremiah asked seeing that Mia was in deep thought. Mia nodded before sipping her water.

"That is fair," Mia said still nodding.

"Mia, I'm not trying to rush you, I just want to at least know that you will give this a try with me. If not that's fine too, I just need to know, okay?"

Mia turned her head slightly to take in the full moment and the expression on Jeremiah's face. For so many years she had focused on getting Cam away from Gino that she never thought to fall in love herself. Maybe, just maybe, it was her turn.

After Jeremiah helped Mia clean the dishes and put her things in her car, Mia was ready to head home for break. Jeremiah stood outside next to her car while she locked up her apartment and walked over to him.

"You'll call me when you get there so I'll know you're safe?" he asked wrapping his strong arms around her waist. She nodded before draping her own over his shoulders. "I'll miss you."

Mia stood on her toes and kissed Jeremiah. She would miss him, too.

Tameka sat still as she watched Baby order a chicken salad with a glass of red wine.

"You're into wine now?" Tameka asked.

"Yeah, it's my new thing," Baby said. The both of them laughed.

It had been about two weeks since Baby and Twan threw the party for Gino and Tameka. Everyone was there bearing gifts and money and Gino and Tameka ate up the attention. Tameka had been playing the perfect housewife; doing everything Gino asked and even things he thought to ask but didn't. Tameka was content with Gino's state of mind and now it was time to get back to the business of things. Tameka's mind went back into revenge mood. She had just come into some information that would aid her in the process when Baby invited her out to Red Lobster for lunch. Tameka knew that Baby had something up her sleeve and it wouldn't hurt to hear her out.

Tameka sipped her red apple sangria and sat back against the booth seat.

"So how's everything over on Manchester?" Baby asked. Since Tameka made Gino's runs that day, he had entrusted her with the pickups on Manchester to lessen his load. He said since she had his name now that she was entitled to a lot more, which meant more responsibility. Tameka was fine with it, she didn't like sitting in the house anyway.

"Everything's good, money is looking better but G is still tracking down the snake just to make sure he doesn't come back and bite us later," Tameka said. Baby nodded before looking out of the window. Tameka kept her eyes directly on Baby. "I think I have more of a lead than he does though."

As soon as those words left Tameka's mouth, she wanted to laugh at the expression on Baby's face.

"Huh," Baby said looking down at her glass of wine. Tameka sipped her drink and smirked, never taking her eyes off of Baby. "Is that so?"

"The difference between my husband and me is that he talks big so he doesn't hear what he should. I learned to sit back, listen, and observe. You know you learn a lot of things that way?"

Baby narrowed her eyes at Tameka before a slow smile appeared across her face.

"It's funny you mention that because that's exactly what I do as well." The waitress came and brought their food and refills on their drinks. Tameka buttered up her baked potato and began to cut a piece of her steak.

"So how's business, Baby?" Tameka asked while enjoying her piece of steak.

Baby bit her lip before sticking a fork full of salad into her mouth. Tameka found her antics amusing. She had never seen Baby lose her composure and although she was still cool as ice, Tameka was breaking her.

"What business are you referring to?" Baby said. Tameka's smile dropped before she put her fork down.

"Since you've been observing and listening so well, I'm sure you picked up that I do not like to be lied to or played with. I've taken enough of it from Gino and I don't plan to take it from anyone else, anymore. So be the real woman that you claim to be and tell me what I already know."

"How did you find out?" Baby asked sitting back and folding her arms under her chest. Tameka just looked at her and Baby nodded. "Look, you know as well as I know that Gino thinks way too highly of himself. Twan is tired of doing all of his dirty work and not getting the credit," Baby started and Tameka shook her head.

"I've known them both for a very long time and Twan is just as conceited as Gino is," Tameka said.

"Fair enough Tameka, but aren't you tired of Gino getting everything he wants and leaving others to scramble after his leftovers?"

Tameka didn't answer her question, but she was passed tired.

"So what does stealing from him do?" Tameka asked.

"We aren't stealing from him. We're building an empire, a better one." Baby said.

Tameka was quite sure that Baby's dreams were way over her head. Twan was filling her head up and Baby was doing all the dirty work, just like she claimed Gino was doing to Twan. Tameka sighed, remembering being that stupid.

"Gino's gotten soft," Baby went on. "Twan has what it takes to do more than Gino ever did in this town and even this state.

"And what's your role in all of this," Tameka asked. "What do you get?"

"Well now that depends on you," Baby said. Tameka knew that she wanted to know if Tameka was going to rat them out or not. Thing about it was, Tameka knew that Baby was smart enough to see that Tameka had other plans.

Tameka knew that Baby knew that piece of information before she decided to confess out of her own mouth.

Tameka watched as Baby took her thoughts for confusion and a smile spread across her face.

"Tameka you can either make this hard on us all, or easy for you," Baby said pulling out a twenty to pay for her meal, "That's all up to you,"

Tameka watched with an emotionless face as Baby finished her drink and excused herself from their lunch. As soon as she was past their table, Tameka laughed.

"How stupid of you Tati," Tameka said sipping her drink, "I almost let you in."

Tameka enjoyed the rest of her lunch in peace before getting back into her car and heading towards the highway. She decided to do a little shopping before she made her last stop of the day before heading home.

Just as Tameka neared the exit, she realized that her car was slowing down. She sighed, almost kicking herself for being so absent minded about the floating gas hand. Making it to the side of the road, Tameka whipped out her phone and called Gino.

"Speak to me," he answered. Tameka rolled her eyes after hearing in his voice that he was high.

"G, I ran out of gas," she said. He instantly started laughing while telling someone else in the background what Tameka just said. She admitted that she laughed too at the situation but now wasn't the time. "G, for real I'm right on the side of the road about to get on the highway to go to the Galleria."

"Well wife I am very busy right now, I believe that's what I pay roadside assistance for," he said. Tameka's nose flared as she tried not to laugh at his tone.

"Sit on my finger and rotate punk," Tameka said before hanging up on him. She went through the car trying to find out how to activate the roadside assistance thing when her phone rang again, this time it was Baywood.

"You're husband is an asshole," Baywood said laughing. Tameka smiled.

"Don't I know it,"

"Are you by that cake place?" Baywood asked. Tameka sat back in the driver's seat and sighed.

"Yes sir."

"I'll be there in a minute," he said before hanging up.

Tameka said a silent thank you, not wanting to deal with an automated system at all. Baywood made it to her with a full gas can in less than twenty minutes.

"If I wasn't married, I'd kiss you," she said getting out and opening the fuel door,"

"Yeah well, you aren't all that cute to me anyway," he joked. She pushed him in his arm as they both laughed. Almost instantly, Tameka realized that Gino had blown her off to smoke. It almost hurt that Baywood was more willing to help her than her own husband, but that was a big almost. Now, it only added to her realization.

"Bay, how do you feel about the way Gino runs his business and treats everyone?" Tameka asked. Baywood tipped up the gas can, propping it up with his leg before pushing his dreads from his face, only to let them fall again.

"I think we all have issues, but Gino's insane," he said. Tameka nodded before smiling.

"You ever wish you didn't work with him?" Tameka asked.

"I've done it this long, what's a lifetime?" he said lifting the gas can more. Tameka shook her head before looking up at the sky. Baywood was loyal. Tameka respected loyalty.

"Teach a man how to fish Bay," Tameka said as she closed up the fuel door and Baywood took apart the top of the empty gas can/ "Don't just give him fish."

When we come up with a plan, we always feel like we have the upper hand. It's so thought out and planned that we see no flaws and think nothing can go wrong. We walk around with our heads held high, waiting for our time. What we don't see, is the person that has done the same thing as us. They listened like us, observed like us, thought like us and planned like us...only better.

"Camryn would you chill out," Mia said getting frustrated by her best friend, "The red shirt is fine."

"You don't think it's too tight?" Camryn said pulling on the long, sheer red tunic that covered her white camisole and part of her white leggings. She then began to pick at her hair, which was pulled up into a bun. Even though it wasn't hot, being 8 months pregnant made Camryn feel like it was still summer and not December.

"Are you sure?" Camryn said turning from the mirror to her best friend.

"Should I do my hair different?" she asked, messing with her swooped bangs. Mia reached up and swatted Camryn's hand away. Camryn pouted before slipping on her white and red Coach sneakers.

"It's not like you guys are together yet," Mia mumbled. Camryn looked up at her.

"Yet? What did he say? What does yet mean?"

Mia looked at Camryn and frowned.

"Are you serious?" Mia said trying not to laugh. She couldn't believe that Jayson and Camryn were like this, "You like my big head cousin that much?"

Camryn sighed before sitting next to Mia.

"Mia, it's like I don't want to be in a relationship because I want to be totally focused on my son, but Jayson just," Camryn smiled before sighing again. "He's just so different than Gino in the best way. He listens to me, I can joke around with him without him thinking differently of me and he genuinely cares about my life and my son's life and not just what I can do for him."

Mia thought about all the things Camryn was saying and instantly thought about Jeremiah.

"Not to mention that when he sings to me, my heart jumps," Camryn said. Mia almost cried.

"Cam, that is so sweet," she said before gently rubbing her best friend's stomach.

"That's why I'm so nervous about meeting his mom."

"Don't worry about it, Tee will like you," Mia said.

While Camryn went on about meeting her aunt, Mia remembered why she had come to see what Camryn was wearing. Jayson had ended up coming a few days early and was at her house with his mom at that very moment. Jayson wanted to surprise Camryn and Mia wanted to see the shock on her face, so she wouldn't tell her.

"Are you about ready?" Mia asked sliding her shoes back on. Camryn stretched her arms above her head before nodding.

"I need to see if Nana is," Camryn said.

"She's ready and in the living room waiting on you," Mia said, smiling. Camryn rolled her eyes before grabbing her small red wallet. She looked over herself once more in the mirror.

"I'm ready."

All the way to Mia's house, she thought about Jeremiah. She wanted to call him, but she didn't want to be bothersome. She wished she had invited him but she felt it was too soon. They had only been talking a little while and although Jeremiah was serious about her, she didn't want to move too fast.

Truth be told, Mia had no idea how a relationship was supposed to go.

She glanced to her right to see Camryn staring at her. She frowned.

"What?"

"You're in love," Camryn stated. Mia swerved a little as Nana told her to watch the road and pray.

"What, no. What are you talking about?" Mia asked looking straight ahead and slowing down to stop at the stop sign.

"What's his name?" Camryn said. She smiled and clapped her hands above her belly, moving around a little in her seat. "I always waited for this day. Is he nice? What does he look like? How old is he? How long have you known him? Why don't I know about him? Has he kissed you yet?"

"Camryn breathe," Mia said and Nana laughed.

"Start talking Mia," Camryn said.

"Okay fine," Mia said turning onto her street, "His name is Jeremiah, he's 22 and he majors in Corporate Media. We've been dating for about four months, he's one of the nicest men I've ever met, and he's a wonderful cook."

"Don't stop there," Nana said. Mia and Camryn laughed.

"We've kissed, but we're not official and I haven't told anyone about him because I'm not sure of what to do," Mia confessed.

"Not sure of what to do? Mia he sounds like price freaking charming," Camryn said.

"He does sound wonderful," Nana said. Mia sighed realizing it was time to talk about Jeremiah.

"Can we talk about him later," Mia said while pulling up at her house. Camryn narrowed her eyes as she saw Jayson's car in the driveway.

"I thought he wasn't coming until Saturday?" Camryn asked trying not to smile.

"Surprise?" Mia said turning the car off.

As they exited the car, Camryn explained to Nana that she would finally get to meet Jayson. Mia could tell that Camryn had developed deep feelings for her cousin. Mia was proud and ecstatic. She had finally gotten rid of her feelings for Gino and Mia couldn't have been happier that her feelings were now for Jayson.

As soon as Jayson saw Camryn, he embraced her in a long hug. He didn't even let her pull her coat off before he pulled her to him.

"I missed you, too," Camryn said before taking her coat off and helping Nana take hers. Mia closed and locked the door behind him.

"This must be Jayson," Nana said with a smile on her face as she nodded, silently approving of Jayson based on first impression. Camryn smiled.

"Yes ma'am, and Jayson this is my grandmother Marie, but we call her Nana," Camryn said placing her hand on her belly.

"Nice to finally meet Nana," Jayson said with a bright smile. Nana held her arms out and they hugged.

"What's all this noise out here?" Miss Kathy said before coming into the living room with Jayson's mom. Camryn smoothed her shirt out before Jayson grabbed her hand and pulled her to his side.

"Ma, this is Camryn, Camryn this is my mom, Natasha."

"It's Tasha baby," she said, smiling before hugging Camryn while Kathy hugged Nana. Tasha pulled back and rubbed Camryn's stomach. She usually didn't like people she didn't know rubbing on her, but she didn't want Jayson's mom to think she was that anal.

"He's a big boy," she said and they all laughed, "Jayson told me you were having a boy. Have you thought of any names yet?"

"No, but Nana and I have been looking at some biblical names and praying about it."

"Ma," Jayson said nodding towards the kitchen. Tasha frowned as Miss Kathy laughed before grabbing her arm and telling her that they needed to finish cooking.

"I'll help," Nana said.

"Nana, we're good, but we do have a pot of tea in here," Kathy said. Nana smiled.

"That's even better."

"You're such a punk," Jayson said to Camryn and Mia agreed.

"Both of you shut up," Camryn said with a smile, sitting back on the couch and putting her head on Jayson's shoulder. Mia smiled at them.

"Are you happy I came early?" Jayson asked. Camryn nodded.

"I'm glad your mom seems to like me," Camryn said. Jayson kissed her forehead and Mia playfully rolled her eyes.

"You two are sick, I'm going to my room," Mia said before pushing herself off of the loveseat.

"She's going to call that dude isn't she?" Jayson asked. Camryn laughed and nodded her head.

Change of Heart

Twan sat on the steps of the Manchester house with blunt in hand. It had been two days since Baby came rushing in the house telling him that Tameka had figured everything out. Although Baby played it cool at the restaurant, they were paranoid. Twan wasn't ready to overthrow Gino yet, all of the camp was still loyal to Gino.

He had been waiting on Tameka to come through, knowing that today was going to be a pick up. He wanted to see where her head was at and why nothing had happened yet.

Twan was very upset with Baby. He knew that she was trying to get Tameka on their side, but she had to know that it wasn't the time. You don't come at someone's wife like that, especially one that will stay down with her husband even when he treats her like a dog.

Twan kept telling Baby to wait until things got bad between Tameka and Gino again, which he knew would happen. Twan had counted in his head and knew that the baby Gino's side chick was carrying was due soon. Tameka seemed as if she didn't care but when Gino softened up and started caring for that child, Tameka would get jealous and all those old feelings she was harboring before the wedding would come back.

Twan tried to figure out how he was going to fix the situation. He thought about taking Tameka and Gino out, but that would leave everyone suspicious with him in their mind's eye.

He had to figure this out quick.

"I figured you'd be waiting on me," Tameka said as she strolled up, her heels clicking on the sidewalk in front of the house. Twan quickly turned towards her but didn't say anything, he hadn't even seen where she had come from.

"What do you want?" Twan asked. Tameka almost laughed.

"Excuse you?" Tameka asked.

"Look Tameka, I know you."

"No, you don't know me," Tameka said cutting him off, "You have no idea what you are up against because you underestimate me. Don't think for one second that you're sweating about what I'm going to do is in vain because you should be worried," Tameka said. Twan had to admit that he was slightly taken back from the look in her eye and the tone of her voice.

Twan took a minute to think about the situation. His gun felt heavy against his skin but the sun was out and he knew he would have to deal with Gino first before anything happened to Tameka.

In Twan's eye, Tameka and Gino were both fools. They both whined about things that didn't matter in the world. They sat up in their big house across town while everyone else grinded for them to eat well. Twan wasn't as bad off as most of Gino's workers, but he felt he deserved more. He had been doing Gino's dirty work for years and years with what to show for it?

"So why haven't you told him yet?" Twan asked.

"That doesn't matter, what matters is what I'm going to do," Tameka said.

"And what is that exactly?"

Tameka laughed before switching her weight to one leg and tapping the other foot against the pavement.

"It's funny how things change huh? I went from being Gino's bitch to running Manchester in what, a few months? You're still stuck making runs and killing people for him."

"I don't want to hear all this Tameka, what are you going to do?" Twan asked, getting frustrated.

"Who is his bitch now?"

Twan stood up and pushed Tameka against the side of the house with his large hand wrapped around her neck. Her back hit the brick with a thud and Twan moved closer to her so that they were less visible if anyone walked past the house.

"What do you want Tameka? I'm only going to ask you a few more times before I decide to kill you or not. I don't have time for you to play because this is not a game."

"Oh, but it is," Tameka said smiling. "It's my game now. I run this and you are going to play it how I tell you to or your life is over. Don't try me Twan, I told you before but you didn't believe me, but don't try me."

Tameka used all of her strength to push Twan off of her. Her strength shocked him causing him to stumble back. Tameka smoothed out her shirt and adjusted her shades over her eyes.

"I'll be in touch," she said as she walked away.

Twan silently cussed as he ran both of his hands down his face. This wasn't going his way and he didn't like it at all. Half of his anger was directed towards his woman, knowing that it was her fault that his plan had been twisted into being part of Tameka's entertainment. He didn't have the manpower to go up against Gino yet. This wasn't supposed to be a war, only a silent takeover. Twan knew that he needed to prepare for battle with whatever Tameka decided to do.

"Always think you know everything," Twan said as he pulled out his phone and called Baby, demanding that she get home before he did.

Baby sat on the couch with a lit cigarette in hand, biting her lip and tapping her bare foot against the base of the marble living room table. She had been home for 20 minutes and she had to admit that she was a little nervous about Twan's reaction to her telling Tameka about their plan.

A lapse in judgment, Baby admitted, was what happened. She had been watching Tameka for so long that she was sure there was a method to her marrying Gino so quickly. The way Tameka reacted at Applebee's left Baby confused. She knew that Tameka would get to Twan and now her man was pissed at her.

She had possibly messed up the plan and cost them their lives.

Baby heard the door slam and shivered. She had heard stories of what Twan did to people but she never saw him in action. She didn't think he would do anything to her.

But she had her razor tucked securely under her tongue anyway.

Twan's heavy steps fell against the carpet as he made his way through the condo, on a silent rampage. Baby straightened her back just before he walked into the living room.

"Do you know what you've done?" Twan said, huffing his words out in short breaths.

"She figured it out before I even opened my mouth, boo," Baby said. Twan raised his hand to silence her. Baby's nose flared, but she said nothing.

"You think you know everything, I can't believe how stupid and naïve you are being," Twan went on, his face getting redder by the second. "That's his wife Tati, his damn wife, the person that will do anything for him and you told her what was going on!"

"Will you calm down? If she was going to tell him she would have told him before even letting us know that she knew!" Baby said pushing her back against the couch.

Twan huffed again, took two steps and had Baby up against the wall by her neck. She winced in pain, the way he grabbed her made her lose control of her blade and it cut into the inside of her jaw and under her tongue.

"From now on you don't make a move until I tell you to. Don't speak to no one, look at no one, or think about nothing until I tell you to, do you understand?" Twan said into her cheek. Baby groaned but tried not to show that she was in pain.

Twan frowned and stretched his arm out, pushing Baby into the wall more and putting distance between their bodies. The blood running down the side of her mouth made Twan's nose flare.

He pushed her jaws together and Baby yelped as the blade cut her more, he pulled it out of her mouth and threw it on the coffee table.

"So you were going to cut me?"

Before Baby could answer, Twan had back slapped her onto the couch. Baby scrambled to her feet to fight back but as soon as she got her footing, Twan's open hand slid across her other cheek.

"You think you bad, Baby?" Twan asked as he continued to beat her. Baby's punches only could do so much. They seemed to only make him hit her harder.

"Stop!" Baby finally pleaded and immediately he did. Twan dropped Baby on the couch and walked away.

It took Baby ten minutes to clean as much blood off of her face as she could to look presentable before she slid some shades on and left. 15 minutes after that, she was sitting in front of Gino and Tameka's.

She silently cursed seeing all the cars home before pulling her phone out and dialing Tameka's number.

"Hello?"

"We need to talk," Baby said lighting a cigarette.

"Where are you?" Tameka asked. Baby closed her eyes before slamming her head into the headrest, mad at herself for getting into this situation.

"I'm outside."

"Jamie Houser," Mia said. Camryn frowned before laughing. She laughed so hard that she had to slide her hand under her belly. Camryn caught her breath before shaking her head.

"No, Mia Downer."

"Ugh, I hated having the same name as her!" Mia said. They both laughed as Jayson looked at both of them confused.

"I don't see how you can remember people from high school," he said.

"We just graduated two years ago, grandpa," Mia said. Jayson pushed her and she laughed.

"And they were way annoying, almost can't forget them if we wanted to."

Camryn and Mia had been reminiscing since after dinner. After dinner, Nana stayed awhile and talked but soon she got tired and Jayson rode with Camryn to take her home.

When they got back Kathy, Tasha, and Mia were watching some reality show. Then Tasha and Kathy went out, leaving Jayson, Mia and Camryn to talk.

"You don't remember people from your high school?" Camryn asked Jayson. Mia looked at him as well.

"High school was kind of a blur to me, but I won't get into all that," he said. Mia laughed but Camryn didn't respond. She wanted to know what he meant by that, but wouldn't pry.

Mia's phone rang and she immediately grabbed for it. She smiled as she answered and Camryn smiled as well.

Now that she was seeing Mia falling in love, it hurt her that she hadn't seen it before. Granted, they were only 20, but Mia had never really had someone to give her feelings to. Camryn was a little ashamed of herself that she hadn't noticed it until now.

"I'm going to take this in my room," Mia said getting up and pointing to her phone.

"We didn't want to hear your conversation anyway," Camryn teased. Mia stuck her tongue out before jogging upstairs. Camryn smiled at Jayson as he wrapped his arms around her waist.

Camryn had to admit that when Jayson's hands touched her belly, she felt warm inside. It worried her, however, that her son kicked. It wasn't the kick he gave whenever Gino was around but it was more of a strong kick, almost as if he was trying to get Jayson to move.

Camryn prayed her son liked Jayson, because she did. Camryn liked Jayson a lot.

"Are you still working?" Jayson asked.

"Yes, but I'm off for two days."

"Can I have you all day tomorrow?" Jayson asked. Camryn blushed.

"Depends on what you want to do with me the whole day," Camryn.

"Convince you to sign up for classes."

Camryn bit the inside of her lip. She had thought about it. Mia had been asking her to move in with her. There was a three bedroom apartment near the one she was already renting and since Nana would be moving in with her sister in February, Camryn had really considered it.

She was so close to being a mom that she was terrified. She had less than a month to go and although the drama she had been in for the last past months had died down, she wasn't sure what would become of her life once her son was born.

The never-ending question of her son knowing his father had burned her mind ever since she woke up in the hospital the first time. What if Gino wanted to be around his son? How could she justify moving away?

"The university has a great sociology department," Jayson whispered in her ear. Camryn wanted to get her bachelor's in sociology. That had been the only class she actually enjoyed in junior college. "You could come up after your Nana leaves, get a job and get settled before school starts in the fall."

"I'm just not sure," Camryn said. She laced her fingers with Jayson's and leaned her head on his shoulder.

Jayson began telling Camryn all of the things that they could do together. Camryn had to admit that her heart was leaping at each sentence. She wanted to sign up for classes the minute Jayson mentioned wanting to be around her son.

She knew better than to make her decision based on his words. Her life wasn't just about her anymore. In her mind, it wasn't about her at all.

Mia running into the living room screaming interrupted their moment.

"What's wrong?" Camryn said sitting up.

"I just told Jeremiah that I would be his woman," she said. Jayson groaned about her needing to calm down but Camryn screamed with her.

"I'm so happy for you Mia, I can't wait to meet him," Camryn said. Mia nodded and kept smiling. Camryn couldn't help but smile at her best friend's joy. It was quite refreshing.

"Ugh, I'm going to sleep happy now," Mia said. Camryn and Jayson laughed as Mia went back into her room and Camryn got up to use the bathroom.

While she was looking at her hair in the mirror, her phone rang to an unfamiliar number. It took her a second but she soon recognized it and panicked. She hurried into Mia's room and closed the door behind her.

"What's wrong?" Mia asked.

"Gino's calling me right now," Camryn said holding her phone up.

"Answer it and see what he wants," Mia said, frowning. Camryn sighed before hitting talk.

"I thought you weren't going to answer," he said.

"Can I help you?" Camryn said, surprising herself that she felt nothing from his voice. It used to make her shiver.

"We need to talk," Gino demanded, "I need to talk to you."

"I'm listening."

"Camryn, I think we should talk in person."

"Gino, you are out of your mind," Camryn said as her heart raced.

"Look, we need to talk. You're almost due and we need to discuss some things before you pop," he said. Camryn narrowed her eyes as Mia mouthed to her, wondering what Gino was saying. Camryn wondered herself.

Although Camryn wasn't thrilled about seeing Gino, she knew that they did need to talk. Whether Gino wanted to be in the baby's life now or not didn't matter, but Camryn wanted to know so that she could be prepared.

"Fine," Camryn groaned.

"Fine what?" Mia said. Camryn held up her hand.

"Are you busy now?"

Camryn looked around the room and bit her lip. If they were going to meet tonight, it had to be on her terms.

"Meet me at the Denny's on Railing in an hour," she said. After Gino agreed, Camryn disconnected the call.

"Do you want me to go with you?" Mia asked. Camryn shook her head.

"No, this is something I need to do on my own."

Gino sat in a booth in the back of Denny's with his arms draped over the table, his right hand slid back and forth over the diamonds on the watch on his left wrist.

He looked from the watch to the Denny's entrance from over the top of his shades. Cam told him an hour but he had made it there in 45. He wanted to clear his mind.

Gino was not too sure of what exactly he wanted to say to her, but he knew that their upcoming conversation was long overdue.

Gino visited his grandmother a few days ago. She had cried to him about having horrible dreams about him dying and demanded that he come visit her so that she could pray over him.

Gino wasn't sure he believed in prayer anymore. It had been so long since he had done it. He slightly remembered wanting to when he pulled Camryn from the ditch that Tameka ran her car into.

He just didn't know how anymore.

His grandmother wasn't the only one who felt his demise approaching. Gino knew that something wasn't right and that when it all fell down it would be catastrophic.

The bell in the front went off and Gino looked up in time to see Camryn coming through the door with her hand on her belly. Gino slid his shades off as Camryn looked around until their eyes met.

She slowly made her way over to the booth and slid into the empty side.

He couldn't help but laugh at how hard she was breathing.

"Shut up," she said while sliding her coat off.

Gino had to admit that being pregnant with his son was a good look for Camryn. Her face was rounder, she had a slight glow and her hair looked a lot healthier.

"You look good," he said. Camryn narrowed her eyes.

"Why am I here, G?"

"When are you due?" he asked, completely ignoring her apparent attitude.

"January 30."

They both smiled. Gino's birthday was January 26.

Gino saw the waitress and asked Cam if she wanted anything.

"I'll have a delicious chocolate shake," she said. The waitress laughed at how she said it before leaving after Gino told her that he didn't want anything.

Gino waited until Camryn had her shake to talk.

"I want to see my son."

"Oh, now he's your son?"

"I'm changing, Cam."

"And how does your wife feel about that?" she asked. Gino shook his head.

"I'm sorry we hurt you," he said. Cam's nose flared.

"Look Gino, I'm trying to move on with," Camryn started.

"Move on? You seeing somebody?" Gino asked as his temperature rose.

"That's…that's not what I meant," Camryn said. Gino saw the painful expression on her face and got worried.

"What's wrong?" he asked.

"Something's not right," Cam said putting both hands on her stomach. Gino immediately threw a ten on the table, jumped out and helped Camryn out of the booth and grabbed her coat.

"What are you doing?" Camryn panicked.

"Taking you to the hospital."

"What? No!"

Gino groaned before picking Camryn up with both hands and kicking the doors of Denny's open. Camryn smacked her lips and gave up the fight. She could only imagine how Gino would be as a father. He always had to be in control.

Camryn was sure that she was fed up with being in a hospital room. She watched Gino pace back and forth in thought and shook her head in disbelief at the whole situation. She had to admit that she liked the thought of him caring for her and their child.

He asked her every five seconds if she was okay or if she needed anything.

That was the Gino she knew.

Her phone rang and she knew that it was Mia calling to make sure she was okay. As soon as she answered, Mia began questioning her.

"Where are you? I thought you were coming back here afterwards," Mia said.

"I'm at the hospital," Camryn said.

"Oh my Lord, Cam, what did he do?"

"Nothing," Camryn said, "The doctor thinks it's just pre-labor contractions." She said. She looked up to see Gino standing at the foot of her bed watching her.

"Is the baby coming? I'm on my way," Mia said.

"No!" Camryn said, "They are about to release me."

"Okay, well call me when you are on your way," Mia said. Camryn told her that she would before hanging up.

"Mia?" Gino asked. Camryn nodded. Gino looked as if he wanted to say something but the nurse walked in before he could.

"Miss Lacey, you are free to go," the nurse said with a smile.

"So I'm not going into labor?" she asked as Gino helped her put her shoes on.

"Not tonight."

The car ride was silent. Gino was taking Camryn back to Denny's to get her car and then following her to Mia's to make sure that she got there.

Gino had gotten a text from his wife saying she figured out who the snake was and had proof. He had to get home so he could take care of this once and for all.

Camryn thanked him when he pulled up next to her car. Before she could get out, Gino locked the door.

"Gino look," she panicked.

"Camryn just listen to me for a minute," he said, beginning to get frustrated with her. He knew that he had caused her a lot of pain but he didn't want her to be scared of him.

Gino waited until Camryn sat back and sighed.

"I've done a lot wrong Camryn and I can honestly say I only regret one thing," he said looking directly at her. She batted her eyelashes and tears glossed her eyes.

"Gino, don't do this," Camryn said. He pulled her hand to make her look at him.

"I'm sorry I did this to you, I messed up your life. You are so much more than I gave your credit for," Gino said.

"G, I'm over it," Camryn said trying to pull away.

"But I'm not. Camryn you were right that day at your house when you said I loved you. I love you and my son."

Camryn broke down and told Gino that she hated him for what had happened to her in the last eight months.

"You've been going to that church with your grandmother right?" Gino asked. Camryn sniffed and nodded. "What does your pastor say about forgiveness?"

"He says that we have to forgive others because God forgave us. And if He forgave us, who are we to hold grudges on someone else." Camryn mumbled wiping her face with her hands. "That holding grudges keeps us from having blessed lives."

"Camryn I'm sorry, but I'm sure that now is that time for you to live," Gino said putting both of his hands on Camryn's belly. He looked down at it for a second because their son was kicking. "Something bad is going to happen to me. I don't know what is going on but I need you to forgive me and live your life."

"G, what's going on?" Camryn said.

"Promise me," Gino said slightly shaking Camryn's arms. She nodded while trying not to cry.

Gino sped down the highway while pulling a blunt from his lips. He had made sure Camryn got to Mia's safely and now it was time to handle business.

"Meka!" he yelled as he came through the door.

"Hello, husband of mine," Tameka said walking through the kitchen with a bag of ice on her eye. Gino frowned at her appearance and once she got close enough to him, he examined her face.

"What the hell?" he asked after kissing her. She kissed him again before moving towards the living room. "I can't hear you."

"I caught Baby stealing from Manchester," Tameka said plopping down on the couch and turning the television on. "I stopped and she swung on me so I had to handle it."

Gino smirked at how cool Tameka was acting.

"My little gangsta, wait did you say Baby?" Gino said as if his heart stopped. Tameka nodded before looking at him out of the corner of his eye. Gino's temperature rose as he put two and two together. Baby hadn't been around that long for her to be the snake. She had to be working for someone. Someone that knew Gino's camp like the back of his hand. Someone that Gino would never suspect to do him wrong. Someone who could get away with it.

"He's been playing you," Tameka said turning to face Gino. "Twan has been stashing money at his place and he ain't just stealing. He's planning to take over."

"What?" Gino yelled standing up. Tameka nodded slowly. "Where are you getting this?"

"Think about it, G!" Tameka said standing up as well, "Ever since he got with Baby, he's been doing his own thing. When is the last time you actually worked with him, huh?"

Gino looked around his living room and realized that his wife was right. The last few months had been really hectic. Whenever Gino did actually hit the streets to supervise his business, Baywood was with him, not Twan.

He felt his veins popping as blood rushed to his head. Gino fumed at the fact that the one person who he would never expect to turn on him, was the one that was plotting his failure all along.

"So what are you going to do?" Tameka said shaking her leg. Gino frowned at her impatient attitude before running his hand down his fade.

"Who else knows?" he asked pulling his cell phone from his pocket and walking to the back of the house to his gun closet with Tameka on his heels.

"Just Chase, I called him to help me out," Tameka said. Gino stopped and turned to face her.

"Help you out with what?"

Tameka looked towards the door the led to the garage with a grin on her face.

Gino shook his head before closing the closet.

"Tameka, what did you do?" he asked pacing towards the door.

"It's not what you think."

"Did you kill her?"

"I said it's not what you think," Tameka giggled. "She's just tied up in the truck."

Gino swung the garage door open and walked around to the back of his Lincoln truck. The tint blocked his vision so he glared at Tameka, who hit the unlock button on the keys. Gino pulled the door open and as soon as he did Baby's head fell off the end of the seat and rolled against the side as if her neck was broke. She was bruised up but nothing major and rope was secured around her wrists and ankles.

Baby groaned and rolled her eyes, mumbling that she was just doing what she was told. Gino pushed her back into the truck and shut the door.

"Did she tell you where he was at?" Gino asked.

"Yep," Tameka said with a smile.

"Lock up the house and let's go."

Tameka shook her head and smiled harder.

"I have a plan."

Mia looked around her room as Camryn finally calmed down. She had been there for about ten minutes and told her everything that happened with Gino.

Mia wasn't surprised.

She wasn't stupid, she knew that Gino felt something for her best friend, but she was sure that he was too selfish to admit it until now, when it seemed that his reign would be ending. Mia wouldn't put an 'I told you so' in Camryn's pain, though. That wasn't what a best friend did.

"It's going to be fine," Mia said.

"What do you think is going to happen?" Camryn asked.

"I don't think that's even important right now," Mia said, "My Godson is."

Camryn and Mia both smiled. Camryn looked down at Mia's phone and sighed.

"I'm sorry Mia, call your boo back."

"No, he can wait," Mia said. Camryn smiled before scooting off of Mia's bed.

"Call him back, can't have you neglecting him already dang what type of girlfriend are you?" Camryn said. She giggled as Mia tossed a pillow at her on her way out of the room. Mia got comfortable on her bed again and called Jeremiah back.

He let out a sigh as soon as he answered.

"What's wrong?" Mia asked.

"I wished you come back already," he said. Mia laughed before telling him she had only been gone for two days.

"I think you told me yes while you were gone just to make me suffer," he said. Mia smiled. She did hate the fact that she had answered him over the phone, but she just couldn't wait any longer. "How's your girl?"

"She's good, with my cousin now in the living room," Mia said.

"Tell me about your room."

"What?"

"Paint me a picture, so I can be there," he said. Mia's face felt hot as she smiled harder. She didn't know if he was running game on her or not, but she liked it nonetheless.

"This is scary," Mia.

"What is?"

"The fact that I'm actually sitting up here missing you," Mia said. "I've never done that."

"I'll take that as a good thing," Jeremiah said. Mia smiled.

"You should."

When you let go of others' worries, dramas and situations, you began to see your own opportunities that were always there. You have more time to love, learn and live your own life. It's amazing how you don't see how involved you are in someone else's life, until you step back, and look.

Tameka set on their couch and listened while Gino made calls to a few of his men. The word was out that

Twan was the snake and anyone that was in on it with him would be dealt with tonight.

Gino only called Chase and Baywood, knowing that he could trust them.

In his mind, after he thought about it, Gino had always known that Twan wasn't as loyal as he seemed. He always seemed to take interest in anything that caused Gino to stress. Whether it was his dealings with Camryn or not having a good business week, Gino remembered Twan being extremely happy around those times.

Tameka watched him. She watched him hard. Every move he made was documented in her mind. She had to know what was going on down to the millisecond. Nothing could go past her because it would leave room for mistakes or errors in her plan.

Her heart was hurt and her mind has switched completely from being in love to wanting revenge. Revenge had been the very thing that had motivated her for the last few months and now that her mission was close to being finished, she could taste it.

Tameka thought that she would want to back out of it by now, let him handle things his way and be the good little wife that she had been, but it was quite the opposite. She could see her future clearly and it, surprisingly, didn't entail her being Gino's wife.

She fingered her ring and her mind cried, it was a few years and tears too late.

"Meka, baby."

She looked up to see him staring into her eyes. She shivered.

"What's good?"

"Thanks for looking out for me," he said. Tameka smiled.

"No problem baby."

Tameka's cell phone rang and Lori's name popped up. She sighed before hitting send.

"Hello?"

"What the hell are you doing? Tameka tell me you don't have that girl tied up?"

"Let me handle this, I should have known Chase was going to tell you," Tameka said.

"You're right, somebody has to be the voice of reason. Why don't you let Gino handle this," Lori said. Tameka's nose flared at Lori's tone. She knew that she was just trying to look out for her as she has always done, but Tameka felt Lori was overstepping her boundaries.

Of course Tameka didn't tell Lori her plan. All she would do was try and talk her out of it. There was nothing left to discuss.

"I have to go, Lo, I'll call you later," Tameka said, hanging up before Lori could get another word in.

Gino had moved all the cars out of the garage. Tameka helped him tie Baby to a chair in the basement. He knew that Twan would come looking for her soon, but this would all end tonight.

Gino sat in front of her while Tameka made sure the rest of the house was locked and secured. One door in the garage that led to the basement was left unlocked.

He watched her intently while she groaned and tried to figure out where she was. He smirked once her eyes finally met his and her lip tightened.

"You put him up to it, didn't you?" Gino asked. Baby stared at him for a few minutes before her eyelids narrowed and her shoulders hunched.

"You are so played out," Baby said looking Gino up and down, "He was going to do it whether I helped or not."

"Oh yeah? What would have been in it for you?" Gino asked.

"I'm satisfied just to see you fall."

Gino's nose flared as he stared at her expressionless face. Had it been a few months ago, she probably would have been lying in her own blood by now.

"I'm curious, where were you two planning to go?" Gino said folding his arms, his gun hitting his side. "I know you didn't think you'd run me out of my own city?"

"Does it matter now?" Baby spat. Gino shrugged. His cell phone rang and he talked a few minutes with Baywood about what was going on.

Baywood told him that Jay and Afton had the spots covered and so far, the word hadn't gotten out to their customers that Twan was the snake. Everything was smooth as it could be. Gino nodded before hanging up the phone.

"If I were you, I'd be careful of who I put my trust in," Baby said.

Gino frowned and wondered what truth lied behind her statement. To him, the person he thought he could trust the most had done him wrong, what was to say of everyone else?

Before either of them could speak, Tameka walked through the side door and locked it behind her. Her chest was rising and falling quickly, making it evident that she had been running.

"There's a black jeep outside, babe," she said jogging to Gino's side. "I think it's our special guest," she said smiling at Baby, who just rolled her eyes. Gino licked his lips as Twan's number popped up on his phone. He smirked before answering.

"How's business?" Gino answered. A deep chuckle sounded from the other end.

"Business."

"So this is what we've come to huh?" Gino said shaking his head, not believing that he was about to go to war with his best friend. This fight would definitely end in someone dying.

"It was always like this," Twan said. "You were just too busy being the almighty Gino to see what was in your face."

"Excuse me?"

"G, you treat your people like they are the dirt on the bottom of your shoes. You been this way forever and it may have worked to get you there but I'm tired of doing your dirty work and you reaping the benefits." Twan said.

"Is that what this is about? You're jealous? I've taken care of you for years and this is how you repay me!" Gino said, now furious. He had been feeding and teaching Twan since they were teenagers. So what if he didn't treat everyone great. He never treated Twan wrong.

"Cut the talk and come out and play," Twan said.

"How about you find a way in here and hope I don't kill your girl first," Gino said before flipping his phone closed.

"Well that sounded like it went well," Baby said. Both Gino and Tameka looked at her. "What am I supposed to be scared because you have a gun? Death doesn't scare me. It's life that people can't handle," Baby said. Tameka nodded. Gino shook his head.

"It's a shame you got mixed up in all this, I could have used you," Gino said.

"Used her for what?" Tameka asked. Gino laughed a little before pulling Tameka down on his lap.

"Shut up, I wasn't talking like that," he said kissing her. Tameka's back stiffened a little before she relaxed and let Gino place playful kisses on her lips and neck.

Baby glared at them before noise was heard towards the back door of the house.

"What's behind door number one?" Tameka said and Gino laughed. They knew that Twan had tried to go to the back door and would soon make his way around to the garage so Tameka got up from Gino's lap and went to her designated spot in one of the corners of the basement.

Gino was sure that how quiet it was, Twan was near the door. He cocked his gun and pointed it directly at the door frame. Tameka cocked her gun but held it at her side. Gino watched Baby as she opened her mouth, but he pulled another gun from his waist and pointed it at her forehead.

"Shut up," he mouthed. She huffed but said nothing.

Twan opened the door with his gun leading the way. He smirked before asking Baby was she okay.

"I wouldn't be worried about her," Gino said. "Tameka, call Chase and Baywood," he said as his nose flared. "Tell them to come clean up in 20."

"So who's staying alive?" Twan asked. Gino didn't respond. "It doesn't have to end like this, brah. You can step down and walk away. Take the money you got stashed here and dip."

Gino laughed as Tameka and Baby watched on, anticipating their man's next move.

"You ungrateful ass, after all I've done for you," Gino spat.

"All you've done for me? I made you who you are!" Twan said. "I spilled blood for you, hustled hard for you. When dudes hated on you, I handled it. When you couldn't control your bitches, I did! I made you."

"All this talking is for the birds," Gino said.

One shot was fired off and the war started. Gino ducked around boxes and his safe while Tameka pulled Baby and her chair behind the metal shelves closer to the wall.

"Why are you hiding?" Twan asked as he riddled the safe door with bullets.

Gino pushed his empty clip out and pulled one from his waist, sliding it in place before the old one even hit the ground. His mind flashed, causing him to freeze. His heart sped up as his moment with Camryn only a few hours ago at Denny's slid through his thoughts. He heard the prayer that his grandmother prayed over him.

At that moment, Gino felt something pierce his neck. His body felt hot as he saw visions of the horrible wrath he had unleashed on his city, on his own people. He felt how he treated everyone, but especially felt Camryn's pain. His Camryn. As another bullet filled his chest with hot metal, Gino thought about his babies. He didn't care what happened to him, but he prayed that his unborn son, and Camryn, would be okay. He hated the pain he had caused her.

Yet, he knew that their struggle had only made her stronger. She was strong enough to raise his seed without him. He remembered when she said that their child had a destiny. Now, he believed. Gino believed her because his was over.

His heart calmed.

This was it.

Something in Tameka's heart snapped as Gino's lifeless body fell to the ground on the side of his safe. She screamed, lifted her gun and repeatedly pulled the trigger. One bullet went straight through Twan's head while another hit his arm.

Baby screamed for Tameka to stop and snap out of it, but she kept shooting, even after Twan fell. She kept shooting as tears fell from her eyes.

"Tameka, you weren't supposed to kill him!" Baby cried as she struggled to get out of the chair, to no avail.

Tameka dropped her gun and fell to her knees next to her husband.

"Babe, I'm sorry," she said feeling his face and chest, trying to detect some type of life. She cried harder as his blood covered her hands.

Baby cried in her chair. Tameka cried by Gino's body. Nothing changed until Chase and Baywood arrived.

When we hurt, we don't realize just what we've decided to do until it's done. Some mistakes we can fix with apologizes, flowers, candies, rebuilding trust and fixing it over time usually fixes those mistakes. And some mistakes, we just can't fix.

Beautiful Zion

December 21

The V4 engine in the dark green 2004 Toyota Celica died down as Camryn turned the key out of the ignition.

"It's almost over," she spoke to herself as her shaking hands pulled at the overhead mirror in front of her. Shocked at the reflection she saw, Camryn quickly pulled a wet wipe from her glove compartment and tried to pull herself together. She learned through this horrible experience that showing emotion caused enemies to believe you were weak. Wiping away the mascara that had made its way down her face, she wondered if coming here was a bad idea. As if everyone didn't know already, maybe her presence would make it worse.

Casting doubt out of her cluttered mind, Camryn emerged from the car as she held her head high. She slowly made her way towards the main entrance of graveyard with the saddened flock dressed in mostly black.

The dark clouds above looked down with a promise of rain on the congregation as they made their way down the old brick pathway towards the tent near the side gate facing the highway. Camryn tried to pace her breathing as her black Bandalino heels carried her closer to her past. Being one of the first to arrive at the tent, Camryn was offered a seat inside in the third row. The large black tent filled quickly, causing those to arrive later to stand around with hopes of paying their last respects any way they could.

"It's almost over," she repeated to herself as the casket was pulled from its final ride by the casket bearers.

Camryn slowly slid the gold colored zipper on her jacket up her chest as the Reverend spoke. It was a very chilly day for the winter season but that seemed to be the least of everyone's worries. As the cold wind blew over the bereaved ones seated in the tent, the tears that had slid down Camryn's brown eyes dried up.

Oblivious to the stares and murmurs of those around her, Camryn's eyes stayed glued to the black marble coffin that lay no more than ten feet away from her. Everything up until this point had been a nightmare for her and she wasn't sure if she would ever wake up.

"Today we won't mourn the death of this earthly being, but we shall celebrate his life. Let us all remember the good times and rejoice that another soul has made it out of this hateful world. Let us not cry for his demise but pray for his eternal rest. We all have our crosses to bear, so let our judgmental hearts take heed at what we believe to be true."

Silence lay across the eerie gravesite as the Reverend spoke loosely of someone he was sure not to have known. Deceived family members, oblivious to the lifestyle of their fallen soldier, shed alligator tears and nodded their heads, hanging on to every word that was spoken. Enemies as well as friends looked on as the coffin was prepared for its six-foot flight into the soil by the hired men and women dressed in black showing no emotion on their professional faces.

Camryn's face grew stone-like as the funeral coordinator began to lower the casket into the cold ground.

"Ashes to ashes, dust to dust."

Camryn wondered if her unborn son knew that his father was lying lifeless in front of them. Maybe he knew that he would never meet the Gino that cared about them. Camryn cried at the thought.

Camryn looked to the front row to see Gino's grandmother sitting next to Tameka, who had been crying her eyes out the whole funeral. She wasn't loud or ignorant with her cry, but Camryn could tell that some underlying pain was hiding in Tameka's cries.

All Camryn knew was that she wasn't a part of it and didn't need to be. As the casket lowered, Camryn prayed that God would have mercy on Gino. She wasn't one to judge, but she sure didn't think that his resume was squeaky clean either.

"Goodbye Gino," Camryn whispered as she pressed her hands to her belly through her coat.

Camryn wasn't sure if it was because of her pushing on her 9th month of pregnancy or if she was really sad, but she cried as they lowered Gino's casket into the ground. Camryn cried hard. Almost as hard as she cried when the 10 o'clock news reported they had found the body of a local notorious drug dealer in his car in a vacant parking lot.

She didn't understand. Yes, he had forewarned her but why now? Why when he was attempting to make a connection with her and their son? Why would he wait until he knew something was wrong before trying to resolve things?

Camryn was scared. Before, it was a choice of letting her son know his father or not. Now she didn't have that choice.

She had to get out of this city.

She tried to hurry and leave the cemetery once the service was dismissed. She didn't want to talk to anyone and sure didn't want anyone to see that she was pregnant and just about due. She didn't even know if his friends and family knew she existed outside of the ones she knew.

"Camryn!"

She froze as her name was called out by Tameka. She inhaled before turning around. Tameka was walking with her arm around Gino's grandmother. Camryn didn't speak when they stopped in front of her.

"Is this my great-grandson?" his grandmother said, reaching out and placing her hand on the tip of Camryn's belly. Startled, Camryn lost her footing but Tameka held her up.

"Are you okay?" Tameka asked. Camryn looked at her as if she had a third eye. She straightened herself up and nodded. "It's okay," Tameka said.

"Are you coming to the repast?" she said. Camryn shook her head no.

"No ma'am, I have to get home to check on my grandmother," Camryn said. She nodded before Tameka told her she would meet her at the car.

"We need to talk," Tameka said.

"Why?" Camryn said ready to put Tameka and all the came with her behind her.

"Can you meet me somewhere?" Tameka asked, ignoring Camryn's question.

"Tameka I..."

"It's really important."

Camryn looked at Tameka and could tell that she couldn't say much in their current location. She rolled her eyes and sighed.

"Fine."

"Meet me at the mall in front of the post office in two hours," Tameka said. Camryn nodded as Tameka jogged to catch up with Gino's grandmother.

Camryn sat on the bench in front of the mall's post office with both of her hands around her belly. Lately, her stomach had been getting tight and her doctor had warned that meant her son was coming soon.

Now that it was about a month away, Camryn had to admit she would be glad to have him here because it seemed as if she had been pregnant for too long. She knew that was because of all the added drama though. She wasn't as nervous as she thought she would be to go through the actually labor, but she figured she

would be in the few weeks to come.

She peered over the Chanel glasses that Gino had given her, before the whole pregnancy, to see if she could spot Tameka anywhere. Camryn had been a little late for the impromptu meeting but Tameka hadn't shown yet either.

Camryn was getting impatient. She didn't even want to come and her back had been aching since she left the cemetery. Right when she was about to leave, Tameka slid onto the bench next to her.

"What do we need to talk about?" Camryn said as soon as Tameka sat down.

"When are you due?" Tameka asked.

"Late next month, why?"

"Gino left us a going away present," Tameka said, smirking.

"What do you mean he left us?" Camryn asked. Tameka smacked her lips.

"You ask a lot of question, just listen dang," Tameka said. She pulled a small key from her pocket and held it out in front of Camryn. Camryn took it and read the number on the key. She was confused but didn't say anything.

"That key goes to a box in there," Tameka said pointing to the clear doors of the post office. "There's something in there for you but you need to get it before the police do."

"Hold on," Camryn said but Tameka shook her head.

"It's nothing like that," Tameka said. Camryn sighed before looking at Tameka.

"What happened to him?" Camryn asked. Tameka turned and looked at her for a second before turning back.

"I'm sure you saw the news," Tameka whispered.

"No, Tameka what really happened to him?"

They stared each other down for a few seconds before Tameka looked away. Camryn could see the hurt and guilt in her eyes.

"Let's just move on with our lives," Tameka said standing up. "We don't have to see each other anymore, you won't hear from me or anyone else. Gino's grandmother promised to take it to her grave. We're free now." Tameka said.

"Oh, and don't open it in the post office, take it to your car."

She walked away without another word. Camryn sat on the bench for about ten minutes before getting up and walking into the post office. Her heart rate sped up as she searched among the wall of boxes and found 459. Sliding the old key into the whole, Camryn pulled out the small black purse, closed the box and made her way quickly out of the post office.

Once she got to her car, she started it but kept it in park, her curiosity killing her.

"Jesus," she yelled as she unzipped the bag to see crisp 100-dollar bills stacked together. There was so many that she couldn't even phantom how much was in the purse. She couldn't breathe. She didn't know what to do, until she saw the small note attached to the first stack.

250 stacks. Consider this child support.

Jayson sat on the couch in his aunt's house, wondering what he had gotten himself into. He had sworn after his last relationship that he wouldn't fall so quickly and here he was acting as if he had no sense. It was a few days after the funeral and Jayson could hear Mia on the phone with Camryn. He hadn't talked to her much since she found out that her baby daddy was dead and that bothered him.

Jayson wasn't one to get played and it seemed as if that was exactly what Camryn had done. The thoughts in his head were that she was using him as a rebound.

He was pissed because he had fallen for her. Her strength in this whole situation reminded him of his mom and his aunt. They were both single parents and Jayson knew what that looked like growing up. He wanted to be there for Camryn. He wanted to help her move on to the next step in her life as a mother. He wanted to love her.

But, he felt his aspirations were in vain.

Jayson wasn't the type to beat around the bush, but the truth was he had been battling within himself about making Camryn his woman. On one hand, she was a month away from having a dead drug dealer's baby and on the other hand, she was smart, fine, and compassionate; all the other things that would make a real man want to wife her.

Mia walked into the room, all smiles.

"What's got you so happy?" Jayson asked.

"Just got a text from Jeremiah," she said. Jayson shook his head.

"You are so simple."

"Shut up," Mia said. "You want to go to the mall with me. I need to pick up Mom's necklace and get a few more gifts."

"Where did you get some money from?" Jayson asked, knowing Mia cried she was broke a few days ago.

"My other grandma," Mia said waving her hand. Jayson nodded, telling her he would go. Christmas was five days away and he still hadn't gotten his mother a gift.

Once they got to the mall, Jayson noticed that Mia went from giddy to ecstatic. She wanted to go in every store and Jayson was getting irritated. He ended up going to bookstore to buy his mom a couple of books from her favorite authors and a gift card to the shoe store because he couldn't decide on shoes.

He left Mia to her shopping and went to chill in the food court.

While he was eating, he heard a familiar laugh and instantly looked up. Camryn and her grandmother were walking in the double doors and looking at her put a smile on his face.

He closed the magazine he was looking at to check her out. She had on some dark denim jeans with a long gray shirt that fit her belly with some gray snow boots. Her coat was unzipped so Jayson could see she had on a long black necklace that matched her earrings. Just another thing Jayson loved about her, she could look fine and just a simple outfit. She was the cutest pregnant woman Jayson had seen.

Her hair was down and bone straight. Jayson had never seen it that way. He liked it.

He didn't even have to acknowledge himself because after walking a few feet, they did.

"Hey sugar," Camryn said with a big smile on her face. Jayson stood up to hug her and Nana, lingering on Camryn for a few more seconds.

"How are you feeling?" Jayson asked, just about forgetting the hard feelings he had earlier.

"I'm a lot better, we just left a church revival and it really helped, plus I have some good news," Camryn said. Jayson's eyebrows slid closer together as his interest peaked.

"What?"

"Nope, you have to wait until I see Mia," Camryn said. Nana smiled and laughed.

"Well, we can go find her right now, she's downstairs somewhere," Jayson said, somehow excited to see what she had to say.

"He's got stars in his eyes," Nana said. Camryn blushed and laughed while Jayson frowned.

"Ma'am?" he asked. Camryn shook her head.

"Don't pay attention to this woman with me," Camryn said walking past them both. Jayson looked at Nana, who held one slender finger up to her lips and smiled. Jayson nodded before picking up his bags and walking arm in arm with Nana behind Camryn.

They found Mia in the foot locker looking at shoes for Jeremiah.

"Okay there she is," Jayson said. Camryn smiled at him. Mia turned to see her best friend and smiled.

"Hey honey," Mia said before leaning down and rubbing her stomach, "Hey Godson."

"I have some news," Camryn said. Mia put down the shoe she had in her hand and Jayson and Mia looked at her.

"Now, you both know that Nana will be moving with her younger sister soon and I haven't decided what I wanted to do. Since I got my associate's here I don't have any obligations to stay," Camryn started.

"Are you saying what I think you're saying?" Mia said bouncing a little.

"I had my store check to see if there were any openings for me to transfer and there is a store about 15 minutes away from that apartment you were telling me about."

Mia screamed as Jayson just looked at the interaction. He licked his lips as Camryn looked at him to see what he was thinking.

"You're really going to do it?" Mia asked.

"I called to set up an appointment to run my credit for the apartment that's vacant in the building right across from yours. Nana is going to stay with me until the baby is about a month or so before she goes to St. Louis. Nana's going to rent the house out so she'll have some steady income. I'm really going to do it."

Mia screamed again, causing all of the people in the store to look their way, but she didn't care. Mia went on and on about how happy she was while Camryn turned to Jayson and smiled. He grasped her hands and gently rubbed the back of them with his thumbs. He couldn't do anything but smile.

He had her.

Tameka made one last round through the home she had so many memories in. She went through the top floor, opening every door visualizing times when she and Gino made love and each exact spot she loved him in. She made sure every closet was clear, remembering times when Gino had her stashing money and drugs in the back of them.

Tameka stopped in the bathrooms, still feeling the water trickling down her as Gino made up for that particular day's fight in their shower.

She made her way downstairs, walking through the kitchen, living room, and dining room. She imagined times were she would cook full meals for Gino and his crew right before they would leave to handle business. Or breakfasts she made with Tia and Jacob, making pancakes for Gino before he woke up.

She slid her shades on her face and ran her fingers through her hair. Following the days of Gino's funeral, Tameka had been busy. Her heart hurt that her love was gone, but she was a strong woman. She would move on.

She cleaned the house top to bottom and Baywood even brought in some cleaning guys to check everywhere Gino may have had something. They didn't want any evidence to come back to them and that was always the routine if someone important got popped off.

Tameka being Gino's wife, everything was offered to her. Legally, she got all his stocks and bank accounts which equaled a cool million. She knew Gino wasn't stupid and had invested his money, but she had no idea he had done that much.

Tameka wanted his son to be taken care of, so she gave Camryn a quarter of it. She knew it wouldn't last her a lifetime, but she knew that if Gino was so wrapped up in Camryn as he seemed, she wasn't stupid either. Plus, Tameka felt it was slight compensation for everything she had been through. It was fair.

Not only had Tameka taken care of that, but she also took care of Baby. She laughed in her head about how slick Baby thought she was. Tameka knew that Baby had been playing her ever since the time Tameka and Gino broke up. She caught on to all of Baby's talk about revenge and things like that. So Tameka set her up, too. Over the last couple of months, Tameka had been gathering fingerprints and strands of hair from Baby. After Baywood put Gino's body in his truck and Twan's in the back, Tameka put an identical gun to the one she shot Twan with that already had Baby's fingerprints right next to Twan. She put some of her hair in the passenger seat to make it seem as if Baby had been in the car the whole time.

They came and got Baby two days later.

Tameka shook her head; she did what she did to set herself free. It was past overdue.

She looked around the foyer one more time before picking up her last bag and walking out the door.

Baywood, Chase, Lori, and the kids were all out front, waiting for her to lock up. She called them over to tell them what was to be done to the house. None of them knew what Tameka wanted to do with the house or Gino's business, which would affect their livelihoods.

Tia and Jacob, who had grown so much over the last few months, ran up to her. She dropped her bag and hugged them both. She would miss them the most.

"So what's up?" Baywood asked. Tameka stopped in front of one of the cars that had all of her things in it.

"Everything in this car is mine," Tameka said before pulling two keys off of the key ring in her hand. "Everything else, including the business, belongs to you and Chase now."

Everyone went silent as Tameka laughed at their expressions.

"Are you serious? I thought you were going to stay and run it?" Lori asked as Chase and Baywood looked at each other.

"No," Tameka said shaking her head. "This isn't for me anymore. I have to find a new life."

"Meka, where are you going?" Lori asked with a sad expression.

"I'm not sure," Tameka said looking around, smelling the fresh air on that cool December day. "But I'll let you know as soon as I get there."

Lori bit her lip as she rubbed her belly, which was in full bloom by now.

"Don't look like that sweetie, I'll be back to visit my babies," she said making Lori and the kids smile. "I just have to do this."

Lori nodded before hugging her best friend and walking her kids back to their car.

Tameka finger combed her hair again before getting into her car and driving away. Three-quarters of a mill would definitely help her find herself.

Christmas had come and gone, the New Year was in full effect. Camryn and Nana were just about settled in Camryn's new apartment and she was due any day now.

She felt better knowing that Nana had been good lately. She wasn't in the best of health but Camryn knew that Nana's sister, Karen, would take good care of her. She was in her forties and a registered nurse. She had been trying to get Nana to move with her for a while.

Camryn and Nana prayed on it and knew that they were making the right decision.

Camryn decided since she was due soon that she wouldn't start school until August. That would give her time to get into the routine of motherhood and her son would be old enough to go to a nice daycare. She was glad that she was able to transfer her job, although she wasn't worried about money now.

When Camryn got the money from Tameka, she went straight home and asked Nana what to do. She didn't know what to do and she didn't want to blow it. She decided that the only thing she would do immediately was pay a year of her rent and got a nice little, reliable car. The rest of the money was put into a savings account for things she would need to take care of her son.

She hadn't thought about Tameka. She hadn't thought about the life she left behind. She wanted to move on with her new one.

"Girl can you please decide what you want?" Nana said.

"Nana, just let me order a pizza or some Chinese, you've been cooking all week," Camryn said lying back on her black leather couch with her feet up. She groaned while looking at her swollen feet. Earlier in her pregnancy she liked the little weight she had put on, now, not so much.

Nana laughed before walking over to the love seat, picking her Bible up before sitting down.

"So what are we thinking?" Nana asked.

"Well, I was thinking Jeremiah before Mia got herself a man with that name," Camryn said.

"Any others?" Nana asked thumbing through the thin pages.

"I know I want his middle name to be Mikel," Camryn said. "Mikel was Gino's little brother's name who died when he was little."

"Is his last name going to be Lacey?" Nana asked. Camryn bit her lip and nodded.

The room fell quiet for a few minutes, except for Nana's fingers sliding through the pages of her bible. Camryn closed her eyes and wished her mom would come back to her with a name for her precious baby.

She smiled as she could see her mother's beautiful face. This time it was more angelic and peaceful. Camryn rubbed her belly as her son kicked.

"I got it," Nana said. Camryn slowly opened her eyes and asked what she meant. "Ian Mikel."

A smile slowly crept up on Camryn's face.

"It's perfect."

"Slow down Jeremiah," Mia said in between kisses.

"It's not my fault your lips are so soft."

Mia giggled before submission set into her bones and she melted into Jeremiah's arms. She sighed in content as his sweet kisses went from her lips to her chin and jawbone.

"I don't suppose after three weeks you are still showing me how much you missed me?" Mia asked. Jeremiah shook his head.

"No, I stopped that yesterday. Today I'm showing you the benefits of being my woman," he said.

"I could get used to them," she said wrapping her arms around his neck.

Once again, Jeremiah had cooked a wonderful meal, but this time they were at Jeremiah's apartment.

"Okay, just so you know, I'm cooking next time," Mia said. Jeremiah stopped kissing her and moved back to look at her face. Mia frowned. "What?"

"Baby, you talk too much," he said. Mia frowned harder and Jeremiah laughed. Mia tried to move out of his arms but he held her down. "Where you going?"

"Let me go," Mia said. Jeremiah shook his head no before pulling her closer.

"I just want you to relax, stop talking and let me be your man," Jeremiah said. Mia wanted to protest but bit her lip as Jeremiah kissed her collarbone. His lips crashed into hers before he asked her if what he suggested was okay. Mia nodded, his kisses keeping her from speaking.

"But you can cook next time babe," Jeremiah said. Mia broke away from him and laughed.

When you let go and let God handle your situations and the situations of the ones you love, it can never go wrong. Sometimes it's okay to be vulnerable, show your feelings, emotions and fears to the right person. When you realize that you had been doing too much for the wrong person and the wrong reasons, it's time to let the rain go. God promises sunshine in the morning.

Jayson laughed as Camryn threw a fit when he showed up at her door in his workout clothes.

Nana shook her head and told Camryn she asked for it.

"I don't want to walk today," Camryn said pushing her head more into the cushion of the couch.

"So why you got your walking clothes on then?" Jayson asked. Camryn glared at him and he smiled. "Come on, we'll just walk the park once and then I'll take you to get some ice cream," Jayson said.

Camryn groaned but sat up.

"That's a shame he can buy you with food child," Nana said. Camryn kissed Nana on her cheek before telling her that she would be back soon.

Jayson held Camryn's hand as they hit the pavement outside of her apartment door.

"How was work today?" she asked.

"I'd rather be sitting on the couch watching movies with you," he said kissing her hand. Camryn blushed before adjusting her ponytail.

"You fell asleep on our movie last night," Camryn said. Jayson apologized and Camryn said he could make it up with that ice cream he promised.

"Oh, we thought of a name," Camryn said smiling. "Ian Mikel."

"That's cool," Jayson said nodding. Once they made it to the park which was near the back of the apartment complexes, the sun was about to set.

They didn't talk about much while they walked. Jayson told Camryn once again how he was glad she decided to move.

"I'm glad I came, too," Camryn said smiling at Jayson.

Jayson was just about to ask Camryn how she felt about them being together when Camryn squealed. They both looked down to see Camryn's gray sweat pants wet.

"Jayson, my water just broke," Camryn cried out. Jayson wrapped his arms around her waist and tried to pick her up. "No, I can walk, we just have to get back to the apartment. Ew, this is nasty. It won't stop, I feel like I'm peeing on myself," Camryn said. Jayson tried not to laugh as they made their way back to Camryn's apartment.

Once the news hit Nana's ears, she got Camryn's bag together and they were on their way to the hospital. Jayson called Mia on the way and she said her and Jeremiah would meet them there.

"He's here."

Camryn laughed while tears streamed down her face and she tried to catch her breath. The reality of those two words was more than anyone in that room could ever imagine.

Meeting Gino, loving Gino, and fearing Gino could not amount to the complete peace that Camryn had in those two words.

He's here.

Coming to grips with the realization that the man she loved from the naïve age of 17 to the growing age of 20, was only in it for himself. Dealing with Nana's chronic illness and her best friend leaving to better herself.

He's here.

Finding out that she was pregnant, almost getting an abortion, telling Gino that she was carrying their child and being rejected in her time of need.

Having a spiritual encounter with her mother and learning that she had a predestined job to provide and secure the being growing inside of her.

Being tormented, beaten, run off the road, scared for her life and the life of her unborn child.

Finding out the love of her life had labeled and treated her like his side piece. Coming to grips with his attempts to make amends and then grieving his death.

He's here.

Right now, it didn't even matter that she had moved on with her life. It didn't matter that Nana in good health, her best friend was happy and in love and that she was possibly falling in love herself.

It didn't matter that Tameka had given her the financial tools to provide a good life for her son. It didn't matter that she was in a better environment to live her own life.

All that matter was the screaming little boy that had just made his entrance into the world, his umbilical cord being cut, physically disconnecting him from Camryn, but strengthening the unconditional love that was already there.

All that mattered was the little one that they had cleaned off and wrapped in the worn, but clean blue blanket as he still stretched his lungs. His eyes closed tight and his hair still matted to his small head.

The joy of her life, the only reason she breathed, the one thing she had protected for the last nine months and the only thing that matter now, was finally here.

On January 26, his father's birthday, Ian Mikel Lacey, her joy, was here.

When God gives us a mission, we may never fully understand the extent of what we've been asked to do. Sometimes we accept the mission, try to figure it out, and do as we're told and other times we reject it, giving rise to an unruly evolution to grow within us without our consent. The great thing is, once we accept our destiny, our fight and our struggle, we may go through hoops, obstacles, storms and fires but in the end, it is all worth it.

Camryn may have been hurt physically and emotionally through the predestined journey she went through, but she survived. God always makes the end worth it.

And her joy lied at the end of the struggle.

Made in the USA
Columbia, SC
18 June 2022

61900681R00152